Letters to Die For

Richard Houston

Version 2016.10.13

Cover Art by Victorine Lieske

ISBN-13: 978-0-9982500-0-7

ACKNOWLEDGMENTS

Elise Abram, for her tireless editing.
Victorine Lieske, for her great cover design.
Deborah Garner for her help with formatting IngramSpark

And special thanks to my beta readers for finding those annoying little typos and plot holes.

George Burke
Candace Levy
Polly Bond
Samantha Blake
And Cheryl Houston

DEDICATION

This book is dedicated to the memory of my sister-in-law, Stephanie Martin, who was the inspiration for many of the characters in this series. Step was never one to follow the pack and lived life to the fullest. Like Sinatra, she did it her way. We miss you, Steppie.

Chapter One

Fred and I sat patiently waiting for Bonnie to finish reading the letter out loud. I'm sure it was for his benefit, for she knew I had already read it. He sat there watching her lips form every word. Then again, maybe it was Bonnie's uneaten breakfast Fred wanted.

"My Dearest Mary, I pray you never see this letter, but if you are reading it, I want you to know I loved you more than life itself. I was hoping to make it through this terrible war and spend the rest of my life with you, but evidently, God had other plans. I have no idea how I died. Was it a land mine, a grenade, or God forbid, one of my own men? I hope it wasn't a mosquito from this awful jungle; that won't make much of a story to tell Mikey when he asks about me. Whatever it was, doesn't matter. What matters is that you know how much I love you and that it's not over. Our time on earth is but a tick of the clock compared to the eternity we will have together once you join me again. Take care of our Mikey, and maybe someday you can tell our grandchildren how their grandfather would have loved them. All my love, Michael."

Fred gave a short bark when Bonnie finished. I don't speak dog, but I knew it wasn't his way of showing sorrow. He would have to wait for her leftovers until she wiped the tears from her reading glasses.

"Oh, Jake, it's so sad. Are you sure she never read the letter?"

"Pretty sure." I pointed to her plate. "If you're finished with that, I think Fred wants it, Bon."

She laid the letter on the table and looked over at Fred with sad, glassy eyes. "Did Aunt Bonnie forget to feed you, Freddie?" she asked and put her plate down for Fred while patting him on the head.

Fred answered by thumping his tail on the floor and cleaning Bonnie's plate in record time.

Bonnie looked up, staring me in the eyes. "Pretty sure?" she asked.

She caught me as I was drinking the last of my coffee. Somehow I managed to answer without choking. "Okay, I'm sure. It was never opened. Debbie, the woman I'm doing the remodel for, says she inherited the house from her grandmother who rented it out during the war, and that the letter must have belonged to one of the renters. She told me to throw it in the dumpster with all the other lath and plaster I tore out. But you know me, I had to read it first."

Bonnie started to tear up again. "That's terrible. The poor woman never knew how much he loved her. You've got to find her, Jake."

"And how would I do that? The postmark is nineteen forty-three. Assuming she was in her twenties during the war, she would be pushing a hundred now. I think she has probably joined Michael by now."

"Then you have to find her children or grandchildren. Promise me you'll try, Jake. Please." Bonnie knew I was a sucker for her little girl act. Even though she would be seventy soon, she could still plead like a seven-year-old.

"Maybe tonight I'll search the web and see what I can find," I said while watching Bonnie's ceiling fan spin. It was a habit I had, to stare at nothing in particular while processing facts in my head. "I can't ask Debbie, not with the mood she's in, but she has a sister. I'll try to find her email or Facebook page and send her a message. She might be willing to tell me something about the place and its previous residents."

"I can't see why the letter would upset her, Jake. Unless it's that time of the month."

I stopped watching her ceiling fan and stared at her.

Her smile made her crow's feet more noticeable. "PMS, Jake. Not that I'd know much about *that* anymore."

"Oh, you had me going there for a minute, but no, I don't think it's that time of the month. She's had a lot on her mind lately. Between the realtor and her boyfriend, she couldn't care less about who the letter belongs to."

Now it was Bonnie's turn to stare – at me. "What's the realtor's boyfriend got to do with it?"

"Not the realtor's boyfriend, Bon, Debbie's. She hasn't said so, but I think the creep is draining her."

Bonnie's jaw literally dropped, and her eyes grew wider.

"It's the little things she says and does, like when she shows me a Tag Heuer Chronograph and asks me if I think he'd like it."

"A what?"

"Those were my words, too, so she spent fifteen minutes telling me how much he wanted a Rolex and hoped he wouldn't be disappointed with the Tag."

Bonnie had been holding her cup so tightly her knuckles had turned white. "He must be some hunk of burning love."

"I wouldn't know, Bon. But I do know he's at least ten years younger than her, and he treats her like crap."

Bonnie seemed to consider it before relaxing her grip and moving on. "And the realtor? What's her problem?"

"He, Bon. The realtor is a guy."

She rolled her eyes before answering. "I stand corrected. Again. So what's his problem?" She put the emphasis on the word, his. Bonnie had been a teacher in her younger days and didn't like being corrected.

"She won't say, other than to call him every four-letter name in the book. Debbie has a real temper and an acid tongue when she doesn't get her way."

Bonnie raised the corner of her mouth, causing a few wrinkles and a dimple to appear. "Must be why she buys her boyfriend expensive presents."

Fred had tired of our conversation, or the lack of more handouts, and went over to the door. My mind was too occupied trying to understand how buying presents for the boyfriend had anything to do with the realtor.

My muddled look must have begged an explanation. "Her tongue, Jake. I assume she uses it on him, too, and then buys him presents to make up."

Fred barked to let me know he wanted out. "Oh," I said, and got up from my chair. "Well, it looks like Freddie wants me to get going before we get fired."

Bonnie grabbed my hand before I could get out of my chair. "Promise me you'll find Mary's children."

I paused long enough to notice her eyes had changed from tired gray to piercing blue, or so it seemed. "Yes, Bon. I promise I'll try."

***

For some reason, the walk back to my cabin on the upper road seemed to be getting longer. Maybe it was the weight of the promise I'd made to Bonnie. Then again, it might simply be a sign I was getting older. I stopped at the small rock wall between our properties and pondered how I was going to keep my promise while I caught my breath. I had built the wall years ago, more as a retaining wall than a fence. It was one of several that served to create level terraces on the steep hill between our two houses.

Fred had been lagging behind, and lay down at my feet panting when he caught up with me. Ordinarily, he would have made the trip between our houses several times by running ahead, and then coming back to see what was taking me so long. "What's the matter, old boy?" I asked, reaching down to pet him. "Are you trying to get out of going to work today?"

He raised his head to look at me. I couldn't help but wonder when the hair on his face had started to turn white.

***

I was dead tired by the time Fred and I made it home from a day of tearing down walls and hauling the debris to the dumpster. Well, I was tired. Fred had slept most of the day and woke only twice, once when I uncovered a rat's nest, and the other time for lunch. Whatever had been bothering him earlier had long passed. All I wanted now was a hot shower and some sleep, but the promise I'd made Bonnie came first. I owed her at least that much, and a lot more.

My first wife, Natalie, considered Bonnie a nuisance when we'd bought property to build a weekend cabin in the hills above Denver several years ago. Bonnie's house was right below us and she'd come to visit, bearing food and gossip every time we came up from the city to work on our cabin. Natalie didn't seem to understand that Bonnie was simply a lonely widow. Her husband had died several years before, but not before taking out a reverse mortgage, so she wouldn't have to worry about making payments he knew she wouldn't be able to afford. She was stuck in her house. She couldn't sell because there was no equity, and she couldn't afford anything in town. Her only income was her social security check. The few hundred she got from the reverse mortgage barely paid the taxes and insurance on the house. Of course, Natalie and I knew nothing about Bonnie's finances at the time. That information only came out in bits and pieces after I'd gotten to know her.

Natalie left me soon after I'd been laid off from a lucrative job as a software engineer. I had stopped by the insurance company where she worked to take her to lunch and break the news. She worked for a local agent who kept a small office with just a secretary and a couple brokers. Natalie was the secretary. The sign on the door said the office was closed for lunch, but I knew Natalie rarely took her lunch hour, so I went in anyway. I suppose what I had really wanted was some moral support, but got something entirely different instead. Natalie came out of her boss's office frantically trying to zip up her skirt and button her blouse. I could see her boss pulling up his trousers just before she closed his door.

We separated shortly after that and divorced six months later. I moved to the cabin, and Natalie kept our house in town, along with our daughter, Allison. I got Fred, a golden retriever puppy, I had bought for Allison's tenth birthday. I cashed in my 401K, my stock options, and took my severance pay then split it with Natalie. I put my share in a trust fund to pay Allison's child support, for I knew I would have a hard time finding work. Nobody wanted to hire a middle-aged programmer, not when a twenty-two-year-old kid, or someone with an H1 visa, will do the work for a fraction of what I had been making. In the end, I realized my heart wasn't in working a corporate job anymore and decided to follow a dream I'd had ever since I had learned to read. That dream was to write a book. Unfortunately, after finishing the first draft of what had to be the next best-selling mystery, it was rejected by no less than two hundred agents. It soon became clear that the book wasn't going to pay the bills, so I went back into construction, a trade I'd learned while working my way through college, and later honed by building my cabin.

I don't know if I'd have made it through the first year if Bonnie hadn't kept giving me work as a handyman. It wasn't until later I found out she wasn't much better off than me. There was no way I could let her down and go back on my promise to find Mary's progeny, but I'd take that shower and feed my dog first. Maybe I wasn't hungry, but Fred was. He always was.

***

"Well, at least the cemetery gives me a place to start looking," I said, and put my plate down for Fred. We had stopped by Bonnie's for coffee and to tell her about my near fruitless Internet search until I had the epiphany to check out headstones at Fort Logan cemetery.

Bonnie had already fixed me a huge ham and cheese omelet, and a smaller one for herself, so once more, we stayed for breakfast. I made a mental note to spend the lion's share of my next paycheck on restocking her refrigerator. Fred cleaned my plate and went over to sit by Bonnie.

She smiled at my beggar and gave him her plate. She had barely touched it. "I suppose she might be there, but I doubt if her husband is. Most Marines were buried on the islands where they died back then. Are you sure you can't find her on the Internet? I thought you were a whiz at that."

"Mary Johnson, Colorado, resulted in over thirty-eight million possible leads, Bon."

Her jaw dropped, exposing missing lower dentures. "Thirty-eight million?"

"Yep, it seems Johnson is the most common surname on the web." I noticed Fred had finished his imitation of a dishwasher and was quietly watching Bonnie. I took a sip of my coffee before continuing. "Then I added the word, obituary, and put her name in quotes. That gave me only fifteen thousand results. Fred fell asleep at my feet long before I gave up at two in the morning, and went to bed."

The mention of my mutt made Bonnie look down at him. His soulful look made her smile. "Still, you'll stop and get me first, won't you?" she asked.

"Are you sure you want to visit a cemetery? It may be after six by the time we get to Littleton. It gets dark early this time of year, you know." I told her how I had searched the Social Security death records and found a Mary Johnson from Idaho Springs whose age at the time of her death came close to what I assumed would be the age of Mary in the letter.

"I've never seen a ghost in seventy years, Jake, I doubt if I will now, even if it is Halloween."

***

I had completely forgotten next week was Halloween. The kids in our neighborhood were too old to trick or treat, and we were too far from town for parents to drive their children, so I quit buying candy and decorating soon after moving to the mountains. It was only when I reached the job site that I noticed witches and skeletons on the lawns of nearly every house on the block.

Debbie Walker, the woman who owned the house, was sitting on her doorstep waiting for us when I pulled into her driveway. She didn't look happy. Evidently, she must have had another argument with her boyfriend or realtor. Then again, it could have been with a neighbor as well. Debbie seemed to have a huge chip on her shoulder, just like my ex. She even resembled Natalie. They were both about five-seven, had long black hair, and still good looking. However, those looks didn't come cheap, for neither were teenagers anymore.

"Where have you been, Jake?" she asked, once I reached the first stair. I had a brief bout of déjà vu, the tone of her voice reminded me of my ex when I was late or had forgotten to do something.

I bit my tongue before I told her I didn't punch clocks anymore. "Sorry, Debbie. Is something wrong?"

She threw the cigarette she had been smoking on the ground and stomped on it. "Something wrong?" By the tone of her voice and the way she rolled her eyes, I knew it wasn't a question. She stood and waved a piece of paper at me. "Of course, something's wrong. The inspector just slapped us with a stop work notice, and you were nowhere to be found. Don't you ever answer your damn phone?"

Fred had stopped at the bottom of the stairs to inspect a Halloween pumpkin that already smelled ripe. He came to stand by my side when he sensed Debbie's anger. I patted him on the head, then walked up the three steps to where Debbie was standing. He matched my stride, step by step, as though he were on a leash. "Why's he shutting us down?" I asked, reaching for the dark-red paper.

"You didn't get a permit."

"We need a permit to replace a few sheets of drywall?"

Debbie swept her long, black hair behind her ears and stared at me. I was caught off guard when I saw her ear was bright red, thinking she must have cut herself. "You didn't know that? What kind of contractor are you?"

Suddenly, I remembered reading somewhere that a person's ears turned red when they were mad. "I'm not a contractor, Debbie. You knew that when you hired me. I'm a programmer. I do handyman work on the side." I didn't feel like adding I was presently unemployed, and that handyman work was all I did lately. I had thought about getting a contractor's license, but that wasn't something controlled by the state. Every town and county had different rules and requirements, not to mention all the red tape I'd be getting into with taxes, insurance, workman's comp, and on and on.

She stood with her hand on her hips, looking at me like a lioness watching a gazelle. After a few moments, her head tilted forward, making her eyes seem half closed. "Get your damn tools and get out of here," she said before turning and walking back into the house.

Fred had been by my side the entire time Debbie browbeat me and now tried to stick his snout in my hand. "Think I should ask her for the money she owes us?" I asked him while removing my hand.

He answered by pushing his wet nose back in my hand.

Debbie was nowhere in sight when we went into the house. I wasn't surprised, for the house was a huge two-story, or three if you counted the finished attic. There were more rooms, nooks, and crannies where she could have gone off to than in a fun-house maze. The house had been built sometime in the late twenties. My guess is it had been started when times were good, but not finished until after the big stock crash, because the upper level didn't come close to the extravagant finishes of the lower level. The bedroom I had been working on didn't have any of the mahogany woodwork, cove ceilings, or lavish touches of the main floor. There were no crown moldings, fluted door trim, or corbels. The walls and ceilings were as plain as the painted pine trim around the doors and windows. All it needed to finish the look of a mental ward were green walls.

The starkness of the room made me feel sad. I tried to imagine how Mary Johnson would have felt if she had read Michael's letter before getting the dreaded news of her husband's death from a telegram. I had found the letter inside an armoire attached to an exterior wall when I removed a drawer to get to the screws keeping it in place. It was a tall piece of furniture, and a little top heavy, so I assumed they had screwed it to the wall to keep it from falling over if a child should decide to use the drawers as steps. The letter must have fallen out of one of the lower drawers and been stuck there for over sixty years. I couldn't help but wonder how it got in the drawer without Mary seeing it. Had she put it there and been too afraid to open it? Or had it been stuck in with other letters and she hadn't noticed it?

Out of curiosity, I went over to the old armoire and pulled out all the drawers. There had only been a couple screws at the top and two more at the bottom when I found the letter. I didn't get to the other drawers that day because by the time I'd read the letter, Debbie had come back and reminded me she wasn't paying me to sit around reading. Well, she wasn't paying me now, so I removed the other two drawers. I can't say I was surprised to find more unopened letters at the bottom of the armoire.

"Are you still here?"

I turned to see Debbie standing in the doorway watching me. She had her arms folded across her chest. "Look, Deb, I know you're pissed off with me, but really, I never heard of having to pull a permit to fix a little drywall. And how did the city even know about it?" I no sooner asked the question, when the answer came to me. "Oh, the dumpster. Of course. I can't believe they have nothing better to do than go around checking dumpster deliveries. It must have been a neighbor who called them."

Debbie started to say something, but stopped and closed her mouth. I could almost see the light go on in her head. "It's got to be that busy-body next door," she said, dropping her arms and turning to leave. "I'll give that witch a piece of my mind."

"Deb, wait," I said, holding up the letters. "I found more of these in the armoire."

"Throw them in the trash with the other one," she answered, and stormed down the stairs.

Fred had been in the corner of the room, trying to sleep, but woke up when Debbie first came in. I could feel his presence behind me. "I know, I should have asked for our pay," I said without turning to face him. "Don't worry, Freddie, I won't let you starve. I'll call her later after she's had time to cool off."

Fred seemed to have a better idea and went over to where my portable scaffolding was set up and barked. "You think we should leave it so I have an excuse to come back after she's cooled off?"

He sat down and I swear he smiled. I knew he wasn't that smart and realized my subconscious was telling me something I'd failed to think of, but I gave him credit for the idea anyway.

"Okay, Fred. We'll try it your way. I'll make up some excuse about not having room in my Jeep for the scaffold, and tell her I'll have to come back with a trailer to get it tomorrow. Maybe she'll have reconsidered by that time, or at least be in the mood to pay us."

***

"And she never opened any of them?" Bonnie asked when I stopped by to show her the letters.

"Strange, isn't it?" I said before sniffing my cider to make sure it wasn't fortified with Jack Daniels. We were sitting on Bonnie's back deck, sipping hot cider to fend off the chilly air. The weatherman had said there was a possibility of an early snow storm in the mountains, so Bonnie insisted we drink the cider. She read somewhere it would protect us from catching a cold. I knew her well enough to know there was more than cider in her cup.

She held one of the letters up to where the sun would be if it hadn't been obscured by clouds. The envelope was so thin it was almost possible to read through it. "Think it's okay if we open one of them?"

"I doubt if you'd be arrested, if that's what you mean. It's not like I took them from her mailbox, but it isn't right, Bon. It's bad enough we read the first one. Would you want total strangers reading *your* love letters?"

Bonnie stopped trying to read through the envelope and pretended to pout. "Spoilsport." She placed the letter on the table and fumbled in her pockets for her cigarettes without saying another word.

I waited for her to light up and exhale before answering. "Then again, it may lead us to the rightful owners."

She was all smiles again and had the envelope opened almost before I stopped talking. "My Darling, Michael," she read then stopped. "That's weird. This is one she wrote. I wonder how it got in the letters from Michael."

I picked up the envelope for a closer examination. "There's no stamp or postmark. Mary never sent it to him. She must have gotten the dreaded telegram before she had a chance to send it."

"You would think the war department could have sent someone to your door when a soldier died instead of sending a telegram," Bonnie said, then went back to reading the letter. "My Darling, Michael, I don't know how to tell you this…" Bonnie stopped again and pushed the letter across the table. "I can't read her writing without my glasses. Do you mind, Jake?"

I didn't bother to tell her they were stuck in her hair, resting on the top of her head, for her glazed-over eyes told me the glasses weren't the only reason she couldn't read it. I skipped over the salutation and most of the letter, looking for names of anyone who might lead us to the rightful owners.

"Read it out loud, Jake. I'm not a mind reader."

I put the letter down and tried not to look disappointed. "You can read it later, if you want, Bon. There's nothing in here for us and I feel like a Peeping Tom reading it."

Bonnie knew me well enough not to insist I read the letter to her and changed the subject. "Well, I hope you're not going to let her get away with stiffing you. She should at least pay you for the time you worked." It took a second before I realized she was talking about Debbie and not Mary. It's not that I'm dense, despite what my ex says, I had been thinking about something in the letter.

"I'll give her a call later after she's had time to cool off. Or maybe I'll call the building department first and see if I can't get them to back off. I really can't believe they would require a permit to patch some walls and ceilings. There's got to be more to it."

"What if it's the witch next door, Jake? What if she knows something about the letters and didn't want you to find them? I'll bet she knows someone at City Hall and got them to shut you down." The excitement was back in Bonnie's eyes. Her crow's feet nearly disappeared when she raised her eyebrows.

I had to laugh at how her mind worked. "That was what Debbie called her. I doubt if she's really a witch, Bon. And I think you've been reading too many murder mysteries. Anyway, I need to find my dog and get back to work looking for a real job. I haven't searched any of the online sites lately. Maybe somebody is looking for an over the hill programmer to fix some legacy code."

"Legacy code? What's that, Jake?"

"COBOL, FORTRAN, and even some C. It's code written in the last century. The new kids don't want to learn it."

Bonnie looked as interested in my answer as a kid at the ballet. "Oh. What about our visit to the cemetery? You said you wanted to check on some headstones, remember?"

"That was before I got laid off, Bon. I need to get back to work or Fred might leave me and come live with you if I don't feed him."

Bonnie had looked a little upset at first, but now she tried not to smile. The dimples at the corners of her mouth gave her away. "I should be so lucky," she said. Then almost as quickly as the smile had replaced the frown, her eyes seemed to grow wide with a revelation. "I could hire you, Jake."

I would have dropped my untouched cider if it wasn't already sitting on the table. "I can't take your money, Bon. And why would you want to hire me? I've already fixed everything on your house that needed repair, and I'm sure you have no need for a programmer."

"Okay, not me, but Margot would, if I ask her nicely."

If ever there were two identical twins that were so different, it was Bonnie and Margot. I suppose if Margot were to remove all her makeup, and let her hair go a month or so without expensive boutique appointments, she might resemble Bonnie, but that would never change their personalities. Margot had the 'better than you' attitude that comes with money. She wasn't in the same league as Bill Gates or Warren Buffet, but she had more of the 'root of all evils' than most. Enough to make her feel superior, and she had no qualms telling you so.

I had already stood up from the table and was ready to leave, but stopped. I wouldn't take a dime from Bonnie if she begged me, but her sister was another matter. "You know how she despises me. She would never give you a penny if she thought I was involved."

Bonnie motioned for me to sit back down and pushed her cup toward me when I did. "Maybe you better have a drink of my cider. I'm going to tell you something about her that you won't believe otherwise."

I ignored the cider and sat down. "Go on."

"She thinks you're some kind of genius." Her smile had become a grin.

She was right, I didn't believe her. The few times I had spoken to Margot she had treated me like the hired help, but in a way I guess that's what I was. She had hired me to edit a book her and Bonnie's father had written, and I had done a lot of work on Bonnie's house before that, so I suppose I was the hired help.

"Don't look so surprised, Jake. Margot's not as cold hearted as you think. I know once I show her the letter, she'll be begging you to find the rightful owner."

"Then you really don't need me, Bon. Get her to hire a real PI. Now, if you don't mind, I need to see where Fred took off to." I didn't wait and left before she could object.

***

It took all of twenty minutes for me to regret telling Bonnie to let her sister hire a PI. It would have been sooner if not for Fred. He had been on the hunt for something on the hill behind our cabin and came running over with a stick in his mouth when he saw me. After our ritual of throwing the stick several times so he could retrieve it, I finally went into the cabin to check my messages. Fred stayed outside chewing on the stick, so I left the door open for him, knowing the chance of any bugs flying into the house was next to zero this time of the year.

There was a text message from my daughter. She had dropped her phone and cracked the screen and needed six hundred dollars for a new one. She was asking me because her stepfather refused to buy her another. This was the second phone she had broken in as many months. Allie hardly asked me for anything since her mother divorced me. Part of our agreement was that I wasn't supposed to contact Allie, so I couldn't let her down now that she needed me. The problem was I didn't have six hundred dollars to give her, and for the hundredth time, I wondered if trying to write the next great American novel was nothing more than a foolish dream. True, I had made a few bucks writing how-to eBooks, and I even had my first novel self-published, but neither one was making the kind of money Allie needed. It was time to call Debbie and ask for the money she owed me.

After sending Allie a text that I was good for the phone, I called Debbie.

"This is Deb. You know the routine. Leave your name and number and I'll call you back if I feel like it."

"Debbie, it's, Jake. Call me back, we need to talk." I would have slammed the phone down, but I didn't need to break my cell phone, too. It made me wish I had one of those ancient landlines.

Fred had wandered in while I was leaving Debbie a message, and looked up at me. His ears went flat at the sound of my voice. "Did I scare you, Freddie?" I asked, reaching down to pet him. Almost instantly his ears moved forward and his tail began to wag. We were interrupted by *Beethoven's Fifth*. I had wanted to use his *Moonlight Sonata* for my ringtone text messages, but at the time I chose it, all I could find was his *Fifth*.

It was Allie asking me for a credit card number. I didn't have a card with six hundred dollars credit left on it, so I texted back my debit card number, knowing it would just about wipe out what little I had left in my account. Now I really needed Debbie to pay up, so I tried calling her again.

"Deb, it's Jake again. I'll be down tomorrow to get my scaffold. I'd come now but it's after three and I'd be driving home in rush-hour traffic. Hope you've had time to reconsider. See you tomorrow," I said to her recorder.

"Well, Fred, that's another fine mess I've gotten us into," I said while going over to close the door. My imitation of Oliver Hardy was lost on my furry sidekick.

***

Debbie's house was nearly an hour's drive from my cabin outside of Evergreen. It would be quicker to take I-70, but I preferred the back way down through Morrison with far less traffic. Big mistake. My seventies-era Jeep Wagoneer needed water somewhere between Kittredge and Morrison. Finding a place to park on the two-lane road with a steep hillside on one side and Bear Creek on the other had been difficult. Then I had to climb down to the creek below to fill the empty water jugs that hadn't been refilled since the last time my Jeep needed a drink. A normal hour's drive took three times that long. It was after six by the time I made it to her neighborhood.

Fred had his big head sticking out the passenger window and would bark at almost every skeleton and carved pumpkin he saw, especially those with lights shining through menacing mouths and triangular eyes. We passed one turn of the century house that could have been the setting for the sixties' Addams Family. The owners had huge plastic spiders, cobwebs hanging from windows, and a mockup of a coffin standing in the front yard with its lid open. I was so engrossed in the Halloween theme that when I pulled up behind a vehicle marked "Coroner" parked outside of Debbie's, it took a moment before I realized it was real.

We arrived in time to see them load someone in a body bag into the coroner's van. "Stay here, Freddie, while I see what's going on," I said before getting out of my Jeep and walking over to some spectators standing on the sidewalk.

An older woman, wearing a red DU sweatshirt turned from the younger man she had been talking to and pointed toward me. I couldn't hear what she said, but knew in an instant he wasn't selling vacuum cleaners or recruiting for the Jehovah Witnesses. He had "cop" written all over. He wasn't in uniform, but his close-cut hair, khaki pants, and blue blazer didn't fit in with any of the other neighbors who were dressed in jeans and sweatshirts with Denver Broncos and Rockies' logos.

"Excuse me, sir," he said as I stepped onto the sidewalk. "Are you the contractor who's been working on Ms. Walker's house?"

"No. I mean, yes, I've been working for her, but I'm not a contractor, just the hired help. Why, is something wrong?"

He paused for a second and looked at his notepad before speaking. I'd almost expected him to answer, "Duh. Why do you think the coroner's here?" but he answered with another question instead. "Is that your scaffolding in the house?"

"Yes. It's why I'm here. Debbie -- Ms. Walker-- fired me yesterday, so I came to gather my tools and equipment."

He proceeded to reach into his breast pocket for his identification. "Sergeant Hopkins, and my partner, Sergeant Cruz up there," he said, showing me a badge and pointing toward the house where I could see a woman standing in the doorway, watching us. Hopkins had been easy to spot for what he was, but his partner was a total surprise. She was too good-looking, in my mind, to be a cop. She had long hair, the color of a raven, and wore a tight skirt that came nearly to her knees. From this distance, she reminded me of Morticia Addams.

"I'll have to ask you to hold off on that for a few days until we finish our investigation. Ms. Walker was found this afternoon, under your scaffold."

"*Under my scaffold*? What was she doing…"

Hopkins didn't let me finish. "Do you mind coming inside? We'd like to ask you a few questions."

Chapter Two

Sergeant Hopkins began the interrogation while his partner, Sergeant Cruz, sat across from us taking notes. We were seated in Debbie's living room, or what they called a parlor when the house was built. The original living room had been converted into bedrooms during the Second World War when the house had been a boarding home until the mid-fifties. It was difficult to keep my eyes off Sergeant Cruz and concentrate on Hopkins' questions. I realized my original impression had been tainted by the Victorian house. She had a lot more in common with the famous actress, Penelope Cruz, than with Morticia Addams. She could have been Penelope's sister.

"You say Ms. Johnson fired you this morning. How did that make you feel? Were you angry at her?" Hopkins asked.

I'd seen enough cop shows to know where this was going. "No, and I didn't kill her, if that's what you're thinking."

Sergeant Cruz looked up from her pad, looking at me the way a cat does when it's watching a bird drink from a fountain. Her dark, penetrating eyes were hypnotic. "What makes you think she was murdered, Mr. Martin?" she asked.

"I... I just assumed that's what this is all about." I hadn't stuttered since I was a kid when my older sister would always finish my sentences for me. "Are...are you telling me she killed herself?"

Hopkins answered for her with another question. "Can you tell us where you were yesterday ..." he paused to look at his notepad, "between noon and three?"

This time, I waited a few seconds before answering. It was how I had learned to overcome stuttering years ago. "I was home, officer, and I not only have a witness to verify that but if you care to check Debbie's phone, you will see I called her twice from my cell phone. And as you know, cell phone calls can be tracked by the location of the nearest cell phone tower, which will prove they were made in Evergreen. And I'm sure Debbie's neighbor has already verified that Debbie was alive and well after I left, for I saw her watching me leave when Debbie was going over to give the neighbor a piece of her mind. You know, if I were in your shoes, I'd be interrogating the neighbor. She and Debbie were not on the best of terms."

Cruz put down her pen and looked straight into my eyes. "Except who's to say someone else didn't make the call for you."

"Because I didn't text her. I'm sure your techs can verify it's my voice and not someone else's." I answered immediately this time without repeating a single word.

I noticed her face soften a bit with the hint of a smile. "And would you please give us the name of who you were with between the hours of nine and three?" There was a hint of a smile forming at the corners of her mouth, making me think that perhaps she realized they weren't interrogating a stuttering idiot after all. She held her pen ready to write my response.

"My neighbor, Bonnie Jones. She lives right below me on Columbine Circle. 3400, I think. I have her number in my cell if you need it."

"That's Evergreen?"

"Yes. Which as you know is an hour from here in a fast car, but takes nearly two in my old Jeep because I have to stop for water at least once because of a leaky radiator. I guess I should have fixed it..."

"Yes, we know." It was Hopkins who cut me off this time. At least I didn't stutter, but realized I made myself look guilty by rattling on over nothing important.

Both detectives were silent for a moment before Sergeant Cruz glanced at her notebook before asking the next question. "Tell me about the neighbor, Mary Jane Mitchell. How well do you know her, Mr. Martin?"

"Never met her, and you can call me Jake. It's what all my friends call me."

"Then how do you know Ms. Walker and Ms. Mitchell didn't get along, Mr. Martin?"

"They had some kind of border war going on, according to Debbie. It all started when Debbie had me put up a fence between them. Mary wasn't happy about it."

Sergeant Cruz tilted her head slightly, waiting for me to continue. Her dark eyes gave no hint at what she was thinking. I wondered if the pause was standard operating procedure. "And why do you say that?" she asked after a few awkward moments.

"Because Debbie told me."

"So you must have been more than a contractor to Ms. Walker. Were you romantically involved?" Hopkins asked.

Here comes the good cop, bad cop routine, I thought. I shifted my attention toward him. "No, not that it's any of your business. And I told you. I'm a handyman, not a contractor."

"So you weren't sleeping with her?" Cruz cut in.

"What?" I asked, feeling the blood rush to my face. She caught me totally by surprise. I found myself thinking, so much for the good cop, bad cop routine. They were both bad cops.

Cruz finally smiled. "Sorry, Jake, but I had to ask."

"Why would you have to ask a question like that?"

"For the same reason we need your permission to take a DNA sample," Hopkins said. He was holding a swab in his left hand. I had no idea where it had come from but realized why the questioning had turned toward sex.

"Was she raped?" I asked, standing so Hopkins could get his sample.

"Please hold your mouth open, Mr. Martin," Hopkins said, ignoring my question.

Cruz rose from her chair after Hopkins swabbed the inside of my cheek. "Thank you, Mr. Martin. We'll be in touch if we need anything else."

I rose, too, and reached out to shake her hand, even though it hadn't been offered. "When can I pick up my tools, Sergeant? I'm sort of unemployed until you let me have them."

She moved closer to return the handshake and surprised me with her firm grip. I also caught a whiff of her perfume. It wasn't overpowering or offensive, but I knew it instantly as the brand Julie had worn. "Tomorrow perhaps. Do you have a business card with a number where you can be reached?"

I gave her my card and left. I had been too mesmerized by Cruz and forgotten to offer a handshake to Sergeant Hopkins, but something told me he wasn't the kind to shake a suspect's hand anyway.

Chapter Three

Thinking of Sergeant Cruz on the trip home made me feel guilty. I'm sure if Julie wouldn't mind if she were watching from above, but it didn't make me feel any better. My mind soon drifted on to the more pressing problem of where my next paycheck was coming from when Fred started pacing back and forth in the rear seat. We were approaching Evergreen Lake and he wanted out. "Hold on, Freddie, let me park the Jeep first. Okay?"

I parked just below the dam, so we could take the stairs up the backside of the lake. I figured we'd have a better chance of not being seen by any park rangers if we didn't walk past the boat house. Fred didn't let the chilly air bother him and jumped into the pool at the bottom of the dam. I was about to call him back when my cell rang.

"Hi, Bon, what's up?"

"Tell that woman you were working for where she can put her drywall, Jake. Margot wants to hire you. She even said she'd give you an advance." I couldn't see Bonnie, but I could imagine her jumping up and down from the excitement in her voice.

"An advance?" I asked, silently crossing myself. "How much of an advance?"

"How much do you need?"

I quickly calculated the more pressing past-due bills. "Five hundred would be nice."

"Hold on," she answered. Then, less than a minute later she came back on the line. "I told Margot you couldn't do it for less than a thousand. She's said she'd wire the money to my bank and I could write you a check on my account. You can pick it up tonight when you get back."

"She's there with you?" I thought about asking why Margot couldn't write the check instead of Bonnie, but didn't want to press my luck. Chances were she didn't carry cash or a checkbook.

"Yeah, we're at the little coffee shop in town. She cried when I read the letter over the phone to her and wanted to come up and see the others. Wait...hold on. Yes?"

I wanted to cross myself again while Bonnie spoke to her sister, but decided not to press my luck.

"She said she'd give you another thousand when you track down the rightful owner of the letter."

I started walking toward the highway to get a better view of the shops. "Great, Bon. Tell Margot I'll get started with a real search once I get home. There are sites that have a lot more information, now that I can afford to pay for it. I've also got some other news I'll tell you about later."

Fred saw me and must have thought I was leaving, so he got out of the water and ran toward me. I managed to find a stick and throw it into the water before he made it ten yards. It was all the time I needed to end the call with Bonnie and step out on the road where I could look down the street to the coffee shop, and didn't see the truck that nearly ran me down. I thanked Fred's guardian angel that he had gone after the stick instead of me.

Once I had Fred in the Jeep, I locked it and began walking toward the coffee shop. I couldn't wait to see the expression on the sisters' faces. Fred was upset I didn't take him with me, but he was too wet. It'd be my luck he'd start shaking and shower someone wearing a new Armani suit.

Bonnie's Cherokee was nowhere to be seen in the parking lot next to the coffee shop. That didn't surprise me, for knowing Margot, they had probably come in her car, and I didn't have a clue what it would be this week. She had a good friend who was one of Denver's biggest car dealers, and traded cars as often as most people upgrade their cell phones.

There was no sign of Bonnie and Margot in the coffee shop either. Its only customers were sitting at a window table and were much too young to be the sisters, so I decided to ask the girl behind the counter. "Hi, Shelly," I said after reading her name tag. "I'm looking for a neighbor of mine who's supposed to be here with her sister. Have you seen two older ladies that look alike?"

Shelly stopped wiping down an already spotless counter and gave me a puzzled look. Then she glanced at her name tag and smiled. "Oh, I forgot I was wearing that. Most people call me Miss or Honey. For a minute there, you had me wondering where I knew you from."

The poor kid couldn't be much older than my own daughter and had probably thought I was hitting on her.

"Sorry about that. Hope I didn't startle you. But have you seen them by any chance?"

She went back to wiping the counter and tilted her head ever so slightly, the way some people do when they try to remember something. "No one matching that description's been here," she said. "At least not since I started my shift at two."

I took a couple dollars from my pocket and put them in her tip jar before leaving.

***

Bonnie seemed surprised when Fred and I knocked on her back door after taking the path from our cabin to her place. "Wow, Jake, how'd you get home so quick? Good thing I saw Fred with you, or I might have called the cops," she said, letting us in.

"Sorry. I didn't mean to scare you, but to answer your first question, we were at the lake when you called. I didn't tell you because I wanted to surprise you and Margot."

"You were in town?"

"Yeah. And you weren't, were you? And I suppose neither was Margot, was she?"

Bonnie turned away without saying anything and went over to the cabinet where she kept her Jack Daniels. "I'm sorry, Jake," she said, opening a new bottle and filling her glass.

I walked over to her and put my hand over her glass. "It's okay, Bon, and this won't help."

Bonnie finally found the courage to look at me. Her eyes were wet. "I can afford it, Jake, really I can. I knew you wouldn't take the money if you thought it was me paying, so I had to make up that stupid story."

She picked up a check that been laying on her kitchen counter. "Please take this and find Mary's grandkids for me...*please.*"

I took the check and tore it in half. Then for good measure, tore the halves again. "You can't afford this any more than I can, Bon. But if it really means that much to you, I'll find them."

Fred wasn't too happy leaving without dinner, but he'd have to suck it up. I knew it was time to leave, even if he didn't.

Chapter Four

Sergeant Cruz woke me the next morning around ten. Actually, Fred had done it much earlier, but after letting him out and back in again I had gone back to bed.

"Mr. Martin?" she asked.

I took a deep breath before answering. "Yes?"

She paused just long enough to make me wonder how the weather was in Mexico this time of year, and if fugitives could take their dogs. "I wanted you to know that you can go to the Walker residence to retrieve your scaffold whenever you're ready."

"You don't need it for evidence?"

"No. We're done with it."

"You know who did it already?"

Another pause. Surely she wasn't recording this…, or was she? "Did what, Mr. Martin."

"Killed her."

"Who said anything about a murder, Mr. Martin?"

"You practically accused me of it yesterday when you asked for a DNA sample."

She didn't hesitate this time. "I suppose we owe you an explanation. She had been found half-naked, so we suspected she might have been raped. But the coroner says there's no sign of recent sexual activity, and nothing to indicate foul play."

"She killed herself?"

"Wrong again, Mr. Martin. I wish I could play twenty questions with you, but I have to go. Homicide detectives have better things to do than investigate accidents. Ms. Walker's sister is at the house and can let you in to get your scaffold. If you have a pen handy, I'll give you her cell number."

I immediately recognized the area code, and started to say something about it, but she hung up without so much as 'have a nice day.'

Fred had come over while I was on the phone and sat patiently as if waiting for me to fill him in on the other side of the conversation. "Well, old boy, it looks like we can go get our scaffold, not that we have any need for it now. Then again, maybe I can hock it so you don't have to go without food next week."

He cocked his head to the side, reminding me of the waitress at the coffee shop. "Don't worry. I have a better idea. I think it's time we sold the motor home we never use anymore, don't you?" I swear I saw his eyes roll.

I had bought the old buggy in Missouri a few years back when Fred and I made a trip to help my sister who had been charged with the murder of her third husband. Except for the trip home, and another to the Grand Canyon to spread Julie's ashes, it has been gathering dust. The last time I'd been inside was months ago when I saw a squirrel making a nest under it. I'd gone inside to see if the critter had chewed his way in. He hadn't, but I'd been thinking of selling it ever since, before the squirrel, or one of his cousins, made a nest out of the upholstery, or a meal of the wiring.

I'm sure I imagined Fred's reaction to me wanting to sell the motor home. The only reason he'd want to keep it is so he'd have a place to hunt furry critters he couldn't catch, and if he did he'd probably lick them to death. I made a mental note to get some pictures and list it on Craigslist after we got back from retrieving our scaffold. But first, I had to call Debbie's sister to make sure somebody would let us in the house.

"Hi, this is Lisa. Sorry I missed your call, but if you leave a message and a number where I can send a text, I'll get back ASAP." Her message didn't sound anything like her acid-tongued sister. Her greeting hadn't been rude, and her voice wasn't spiteful either. Maybe I was reading too much into it, but it made me wonder how much she was like Debbie.

"Hi, Lisa, this is Jake Martin, the handyman who was working on your sister's house. Sergeant Cruz said I could pick up my scaffold, and gave me this number."

I ended the call and looked down at Fred. "Well, boy, think we should go anyway?"

He gave a short bark, then ran over to the door. If there was one word he did understand, it was the word 'go.'

***

There was a late model minivan with Missouri plates parked in front of Debbie's when we finally got there a few hours later. Once again the hour trip took three because of all the stops to let the Jeep cool off so I wouldn't crack the engine block. I really needed to get the Jeep's radiator fixed, or trade it in for something less thirsty.

My little gray cells told me the minivan belonged to Lisa. Not that I'm any relation to the great Hercule Poirot, it's that the 816 number she had called me from is for Kansas City, and the sign on the side of the van that said, "Flowers by Lisa" was also a big help in making my brilliant deduction. Poirot would have been proud.

Lisa was sitting at the top of the stairs engrossed in her cell phone and barely acknowledged me. She wearing a low-cut, Kansas City Royals' shirt, and baggy, tan shorts with big pockets on the legs. I climbed the short flight of stairs with Fred glued to my side. Lisa was too busy Twittering to look up when we approached. I didn't really know if she was Twittering or tweeting. I don't know--or care--what it's called. She could have been on any number of social media for all I knew.

"You must be Jake?" she said, standing up and slipping the phone into one of her pockets, and her reading glasses into another.

"In the flesh," I answered, wondering what kind of cell phone she had, for she didn't sound anything like her voicemail. "Thanks for meeting us. I wasn't sure if you got my message."

"Yes, I did. Sorry I didn't text you back yet, but your name sounded familiar, and when I remembered where I heard it before, I just had to go out and find your book. I've been reading it on my phone ever since."

"You're reading my book?" I suddenly felt bad for thinking she was another social media junkie.

"Yes, it's quite interesting. And this has to be Fred, the wonder dog," she said, reaching out to pet him.

Quite interesting? I wondered if that meant she liked it, or what?

"Say hi to the nice lady, Freddie."

Whatever glue had been keeping him attached to my leg dissolved when she patted him on the head. The big ham sat ever so nicely and offered his paw. Trouble was, the goofy mutt used his left paw. But when Lisa shook it with her left hand, I noticed the lack of any rings on her fingers and realized Fred wasn't so dumb after all. Did he want me to know she wasn't married or engaged?

Her smile caused little crow's feet to form under her eyes. "So you *are* as smart as your master makes you out, aren't you?"

Fred didn't show any wrinkles under his eyes, but it sure looked like he was smiling.

"Well, I imagine you'd like to go in and get your scaffold. I hope you don't mind if I stay out here and read more of your book. It makes me too sad to go into that room," she said, dropping her eyes.

I hesitated, trying to think of something I could say to cheer her up, so I could ask the question that had been on my mind ever since Sergeant Cruz told me Debbie wasn't murdered.

Lisa looked up after a few awkward moments of silence. Her dark-blue eyes had no hint of the tears I had expected to see. "Yes?" she asked.

"I'm really sorry, Lisa. I didn't know your sister that well, but she seemed like a nice person. If you don't mind me asking, how did she die?"

Evidently I'd struck a nerve that led straight to her funny bone and she laughed. It wasn't a chortle or giggle, but more of a snicker. "Good try, Jake. If my sister was nice, then the Wicked Witch of the East was a saint."

"Okay, maybe she had a mean streak, but I think she meant well."

A hint of a smile lit up her face, making me think of the girl with the same name made famous by Da Vinci. I wouldn't call her beautiful, not in the sense the media wants us to perceive beauty. Her hips and breasts would never tolerate one of those size zero outfits worn by runway models, but she had the same mysterious look as the woman made so famous by Leonardo. I couldn't help but wonder what she was thinking. I wanted to ask her a million questions, like how long was she planning to be in town, or if she liked Italian food because I knew this great place on 38th, when Fred reminded me why were there, and ran into the house.

***

"Thanks a lot, Freddie," I said when I caught up with him in the second-floor bedroom where we had been working. Then I saw why he had been so anxious to run into the house. He had a little kitten, that couldn't be more than a few months old, cornered by the armoire. I knew he wouldn't hurt it, but the poor cat didn't. It was hissing and striking out at him with its little paw.

"Fred!" I yelled. "Leave that poor kitten alone and get over here."

He immediately forgot about his new playmate and came over with his tail between his legs. I tried to look mad and pointed my finger at him to stay before going over to the kitten. Unfortunately, the tone of my voice scared the poor creature more than it did Fred, and it bolted for the door when it saw its chance to escape. I turned around in time to see Lisa standing there, holding the kitten.

"Poor baby," she said, stroking the fur on its head. "Did that big bully try to hurt you?"

"He wouldn't hurt a flea, Lisa. I don't know what got into him; I've never know him to chase cats before." When I saw the look on her face, I knew she wasn't buying it. "Honest. Maybe he thought it was a rat. He found a nest of them last week. I'm sure that's what it was."

"Yeah, right. Well, I'd appreciate it if you'd get your damn scaffold and leave." Her tone of voice told me I'd be wasting my breath asking her to dinner. She turned and left, but not before I heard her talking to the cat with a much gentler voice, one I knew she'd never use on me.

***

Fred laid down by the armoire, acting sad, while I tore the scaffold apart. He was pathetic, holding his head between his paws, but keeping his eyes on me so that they looked like huge buttons. He reminded me of one of those big-eyed kid pictures by Keane that my mom used to think were so cool back in the seventies. I only remember the name because I had a fifth-grade teacher with the same name who also had big, dark eyes.

My scaffold is a little less than six feet tall, designed to hold walk boards at two different heights, the first at a few feet off the ground and another at the top. OSHA could have written their weekly quota of violations if they saw my setup. Instead of using OSHA approved aluminum walk boards, I used much cheaper, pine two-by-twelves. The bedroom had ten-foot ceilings, tall by today's standards, but common in the twenties. With less than four feet between the top boards and ceiling, I'd have to lie down to work. That might work for Michelangelo, but this wasn't the Sistine Chapel, so I had stood on the bottom boards, which allowed me to reach the ceiling without lying down on the job. This left the top boards for my tools and bucket of mud, AKA drywall compound.

The first task in breaking down the scaffold is removing all the walk boards, but someone had already removed the top board along with my tools and mud. My drywall knives and mud pan were lying on the floor, but the bucket of mud was gone. I couldn't imagine Debbie taking it, for it had been nearly full, and weighed over sixty pounds.

"What do you think, Fred, did someone break in and steal our stuff?" Asking him questions was my way of talking to myself. "Okay, don't answer me, but can I trust you to stay put while I go check the dumpster? Maybe somebody threw the bucket of mud away." He either didn't understand or wasn't in the mood to obey when he followed me outside.

The dumpster was the kind that was not only open at the top, but also had doors on the front to allow a person to walk in. I thought I had closed the doors the last time I used it but was surprised to find them wide open. Then I saw why. It was nearly full with old couches, TVs, broken furniture, and appliances. The neighbors must have been using it as their private dump.

Fred followed me inside then ran ahead of me and started digging in the trash. He came up with a piece of meat and tried to run past me so he could take it somewhere to either eat or bury. I caught his collar before he escaped the dumpster.

"What is this, Fred?" I said, taking it out of his jaws. I didn't need his answer for I could see it was a ham. The thing that surprised me is it was a whole ham and it didn't smell. When I went over to where Fred had found it, I found several dozen frozen food boxes; everything from frozen pizzas to TV dinners. They were all defrosted, and like the ham, didn't smell. I assumed a neighbor had recently cleaned out a freezer. I threw the ham back where Fred had found it, closed the front doors to the dumpster and went back to retrieve my scaffold. Fred didn't want to leave his new found treasure but came when I threatened to put him back in the Jeep if he didn't come.

He headed straight for the scaffold when we got back to the bedroom and began sniffing around the bottom boards before scooting under them. "Don't tell me you found more food under there? What's the matter with you today? Do you have a tapeworm or something?"

He started barking when I went to remove the board he was hiding under. "I hope there aren't any more cats under there, mister, or you'll get us kicked out of here before I have a chance to get my scaffold torn apart."

He grabbed the end of the board I'd just removed and growled. "Are you crazy, Freddie? Let it go, it's not a stick." Then I noticed what looked like writing scratched on the bottom. I knew Fred couldn't read, so I assumed Debbie must have written it with something edible, something strong enough for Fred's nose to smell days after Debbie wrote it.

He looked up at me with a huge grin on his face. "I'm sorry, Freddie," I said and knelt down to his level, taking his big head in both my hands. "I suppose you think this makes up for chasing that poor little kitty?"

He answered by giving be a big wet kiss on the cheek.

"Okay, you're forgiven," I said, wiping my face before turning to get a closer look at the message. There was no doubt it was written in blood.

Chapter Five

"You have reached Sergeant Cruz of the Denver PD. I'm sorry I can't answer, but if you leave a message I'll get back as soon as possible. If it's an emergency, please hang up and call 911."

"Sergeant, this is Jacob Martin, Debbie Walker's handyman. I think I found something on one of my scaffold walk boards you need to see. Well actually, Fred found it, but that's really not important." I tried to laugh at my little joke before continuing. "Anyway, I'm at Debbie's now and will try to hang around 'till you call back, but her sister might not let me." Once more I realized how nervous I must have sounded by rattling on.

"Are you calling the police?" Lisa had walked into the room, without the kitten, as I finished my message. I should have realized it sooner when Fred had reattached himself to me.

"I think you'd better look at this, Lisa," I answered, pointing toward the walk boards.

She went over to the boards, lowered her glasses, and squinted her eyes. "Okay, so you write your initials on your equipment. You didn't have to call the police. I wasn't going to keep them."

"I didn't write it, Lisa. Debbie did."

I watched as she repositioned her glasses with a single index finger before bending down to take a closer look. "JM. Jake Martin. You're telling me Debbie wrote that?"

"I might be able to answer that if you'd tell me how she died. For some reason, nobody wants to tell me."

She stared wide-eyed a second too long before speaking. "You don't know?"

"No. Sergeant Cruz wouldn't tell me and I feel like you've been avoiding it. What's the big secret, anyway?"

Her eyes drifted toward the shuttered window behind me and she unconsciously scratched her earlobe. "They say it was your bucket of drywall compound. She must have bumped into your scaffold and knocked it loose. It broke her neck when it hit her on the head."

I stood there speechless. Visions of a barbecue grill blowing up in a neighbor's face a couple years ago came flooding back in my mind. The neighbor died and the family sued me for negligence. Could this be happening again?

Whatever itch she had behind her ear must have moved on to her upper arm. "Don't look so horrified, Jake," she said while scratching her arm. "I'm not going to sue you. Brendon says you don't have a pot to piss in, so I'd be wasting my time."

"Brendon?"

Lisa dropped her eyes. "Debbie's realtor. He came by earlier to offer his condolences. I'm not sure how, but your name came up, and that's when he told me about you."

"Oh? I didn't realize I was such a celebrity. Did he also tell you Debbie fired him some time ago?"

"Really?" she said, looking me in the eyes again. "I suppose that shows you can't believe anyone these days, Can you?"

"I suppose, but he's right about one thing, Lisa. You'd be wasting your time because it was no accident. I think someone murdered her and made it look that way."

It looked like her eyes might pop out. At the very least she resembled one of the carved pumpkins I'd seen earlier with triangular sockets where their eyes should be.

"Someone murdered her?"

"I think so, someone with the initials JM. But first, tell me something. Did they do an autopsy?"

"Not that I know of."

"Then how do you know her neck was broken?"

"It's what I heard the other detective say. Cruz told him to wait for the autopsy before jumping to conclusions. So I guess they will do one when they get around to it."

"I wish I could see it. My money's on a brain hemorrhage or something caused by a blow to the head. She'd never had time to write the message if her neck was broken."

Lisa's face had softened some. She no longer looked like Janet Leigh being attacked in the shower, but she still did a good impersonation of Kathy Bates holding a sledgehammer. "So this is what legalizing marijuana does. Is everyone in this state smoking it? Don't you think that's the first thing they'd notice? And how do you know she'd die instantly from a broken neck? I think you've been reading too many Agatha Christie novels."

She had me there. Not on the smoking accusation, I've never touched that stuff in my life, but on the broken neck. "Okay, I'm not a doctor. I suppose she could have broken her neck, but wouldn't that be bloodless?"

Lisa's eyes went wide again, so I thought I'd better explain before it drove her nuts. "Look at that writing. Doesn't that look like dried blood?"

She pushed on the middle of her glasses with her index finger and bent down to get a closer look. "Looks like something broad like a crayon, or a wide marker."

"Well, if it's not blood, it had to be something edible."

"An edible food marker?" Her eyes seemed to sparkle.

"A what?"

"Cake decorators use them, Jake. But why does it have to be edible."

I pointed to Fred who had been sitting quietly, listening to our conversation like he understood every word. "He found the message with his nose. His two favorite things in life are sleep and food. He must have thought it was something to eat."

"Aw, Fred, are you going to let him talk about you like that?" she said and bent down to ruffle the hair on the top of his head.

Fred barked, and Lisa laughed.

"I'm sorry I got mad earlier, Jake. Why don't I make it up to you and buy you two lunch? I'd love to hear more about where you get these ideas for your murder mysteries."

Chapter Six

I watched while Lisa played ball with Fred, and laughed every time she had to wipe his slobber on her cargo pants. Our lunch consisted of a bucket of the Colonel's finest, with a pint of mashed potatoes, and another of coleslaw, that we took to a nearby park. Denver was experiencing unusually warm temperatures for October and I had suggested the park when asked where I'd like to eat. Fred wasn't welcome at most restaurants.

She finally tired of the game and came back to the picnic bench. "Doesn't he ever get tired?" she asked before sitting down.

"I'm afraid the ball will wear out before he does," I answered, unconsciously picking off a piece of meat from the thigh I had been eating, and throwing it to Fred.

She watched him eat the chicken in a single gulp. If she disapproved, I couldn't see it in her face, for she simply stared as though she was lost in other thoughts. "Jake, I was wondering," she said after turning back to me but paused again. "I was wondering if you would hold off telling the police about those initials."

I had a mouth full of chicken and had to wash it down with a sip of soda before I could speak. She smiled politely and continued. "I mean, it's not much of a reason to suspect murder, is it? And I really need to get back to Kansas City by the end of the week. If you make them suspect it's not an accident then I could be tied up here for months and lose my job."

I finally swallowed the chicken and found my voice. "Are you asking me to ignore the possibility that your sister was murdered?"

"No, of course not. But please think of the consequences, Jake. I'm not a rich woman, and I really need my job. Debbie didn't care much about family and left me to take care of our mother. I can't do that without an income."

"But you can't let the murderer just walk away, and besides, don't you own the business?"

She looked at me blankly.

"The sign on your minivan. It says 'Flowers by Lisa', I assumed that's you."

"Oh, right," she said. "I've been meaning to have that removed and haven't got around to it. I'm afraid that went broke some time ago, and now I work the front desk of a friend's law firm."

She reached out and placed her right hand on my arm. "I'm not asking you to let someone get away with murder, silly, but at least get better evidence than some scribbling on a piece of wood before you raise the alarm. For starters, who would *want* to kill her?"

Her touch and soft voice had its effect. I found myself staring into her dark eyes wondering if I'd be lucky enough to see her again if I refused her plea, but Fred had other ideas and broke the spell with a loud bark.

"I think he wants the rest of that chicken," Lisa said, removing her hand from my arm and forcing a laugh.

I pulled the rest of the meat from the chicken and gave it to Fred. Lisa wasn't smiling when I looked up to answer. "Maybe it was that acid tongue you mentioned that got her killed. She might have pissed off someone just enough to pick up a hammer or something and hit her with it. Come to think of it, I overheard her in more than one heated argument with her boyfriend. He was always hitting her up for money. Then maybe it was her next door neighbor. She didn't like all the noise and mess I was making. Debbie thought she might have been the one who got the stop work order. Or it could have been something as simple as a burglary gone bad."

"Or it could be an accident, just like the police said." She took a slow, deep breath before continuing, "If you manage to get them to think otherwise, my job will be long gone by the time they track down all those leads."

I couldn't think of a comeback. It was obvious she didn't want me sticking my nose into Debbie's death and made me wonder what she really had to gain from letting it go as an accident. If I didn't know any better, I'd think *she* killed her sister, but she was still in Kansas City when Debbie died. Unless she had psychokinetic powers, there was no way she could have managed to put the dent in Debbie's head that killed her.

She must have realized my hesitation meant I wasn't buying her plea. "Tell you what, Jake," she said, leaning in a little too close, "how about I help you track down some of those leads?" Her lips formed a slight smile and reminded me of the car salesman a few years back who tried to sell me a good used Yugo with only two hundred thousand miles. "There won't be a service for Debbie. She had no friends I know of, so I should be able to wrap up the funeral arrangements and have a few days left over to help you. I could start by talking to that neighbor and maybe the realtor."

Maybe I'd misread her smile, for now she had the look of a little girl begging her daddy for a pony. "Then you agree it might be more than an accident?" I asked.

Her hand was back on my arm. "No, but how can I argue with a guy with such beautiful, eyes? Did anyone ever tell you they look like columbines?"

"Colorado's state flower? No they haven't. And I'm not going to tell you that yours are like flowering hawthorns."

She looked puzzled. "Flowering hawthorns? Why would you say that?"

"Sorry, bad joke. They're Missouri's state flower."

Her grip on my arm seemed to tighten. "Oh, now I get it."

Without warning, Fred tried to force his tennis ball into Lisa's free hand, breaking the spell she had been casting. "Oh, Freddie, have I been ignoring you?" she said, releasing my arm so she could take the ball and throw it for him.

Chapter Seven

"I think she likes you, Jake," Bonnie said when I told her about Lisa the next morning. She had been holding her coffee with two hands, trying to get warm. We were sitting on her deck because the sun was out, and it was supposed to reach seventy in Denver, but it was much colder at nearly eight thousand feet.

"Maybe. Or maybe she's trying to sell me a Yugo."

Bonnie looked at me like I'd just escaped the mental hospital in Pueblo.

"A car from Yugoslavia they tried to sell here in the eighties. Calling it a lemon would be too kind," I said.

Her lips turned up slightly at the corners. She must have realized I wasn't ready for the funny farm quite yet. "Oh, so you think it was all an act to get you to drop the murder investigation?"

"I did, but then she offered to help me. Talk about a mixed up female."

Bonnie crossed her arms before speaking. She was no longer smiling. "And men never change their minds?"

"Sorry, Bon. Hold on a minute while I extract my foot from my mouth."

A smile betrayed her attempt at anger, so I continued. "It's the way she offered to help. Telling me I had columbine eyes and squeezing my arm. I didn't know if I should kiss her or what."

"I think your hormones are affecting your brain, Jake. It's obvious she's worried about losing her job and doesn't want you stirring things up." Then I saw a gleam in her eyes that I hadn't seen since last year when she had helped me solve another murder. "But we could check into it without her knowing." She looked like someone who just won the lotto.

"We?" I asked.

"Of course, Jake. We're a team whether you want to admit it or not. Like Tommy and Tuppence, or Nick and Nora."

"I've seen enough Thin Man movies to know who Nick and Nora Charles are, but who on earth are Tommy and Tuppence?"

Bonnie picked up her cup and sat back holding it in both hands again. "You really need to read more Agatha Christie if you want to write mysteries, Jake. But never mind them, they didn't have a dog. I think Fred could be as good as Asta, Don't you?"

Fred had been lying on the deck under Bonnie's table and raised his head at the mention of his name.

"How about it, Freddie? Can we change your name to Asta?"

He tipped his head to one side and gave me a look that was a lot like the one Bonnie had when she thought I'd escaped from Pueblo.

"What? Of course, Fred. I should have thought of that," I said before turning back to Bonnie. "He says you remind him of Miss Marple."

She was about to take a sip of her coffee but laughed instead before answering. "But surely he agrees the three of us make a great team."

"Yes. I should know better than try to talk you out of something once you've made up your mind. Lisa said she'd check the alibis of the neighbor and realtor, so that leaves the boyfriend for us. But there's another lead I didn't mention to Lisa." I waited long enough to be dramatic.

Bonnie lifted her left eyebrow and stared at me. "So, are you going to tell me?"

"The letter, Bon. The one Mary wrote before she knew Michael was dead. Didn't you find it a little strange?"

"I thought you only skimmed over it. Did I miss something?"

"Unless she had the gestation period of an elephant, the baby she mentioned couldn't be Michael's. He'd been overseas for thirteen months when the child was born. It might also explain why she never mailed the letter."

Bonnie's eyes went wide. "She was too ashamed to tell him the baby wasn't his. So, what's that got to do with Debbie being murdered?"

"Probably nothing, but what if the child is some big shot now, like a clergyman or a politician, wouldn't he want to keep something like that quiet?"

"Or she. Women can be preachers and politicians, too, you know."

"Yes, Bon, I know. And they can murder as well."

Bonnie saw my cup was empty and reached for an insulated carafe sitting on the table. "Maybe we should leave well enough alone, Jake. If that's true, I'm glad you didn't let me pay you to find Mary's children," she said while refilling my cup.

I didn't object to the coffee even though I'd had enough. Her remark made me think about how quickly people change. Only two days ago she created an elaborate lie to get me to find Mary's kids, and now she was having second thoughts. "Even if he or she killed to keep it quiet?" I asked.

"Well, no, but what if he didn't do it and you're right about him being some kind of VIP? I can't see where dragging all that out in the open will do anyone any good."

"Now it's he, is it?"

She sat back in her chair and crossed her arms. "You know what I mean," she said before locking her lips together tighter than a rusted pair of vice grips.

"Sorry, Bon. How about I make it up to you and buy you lunch after I run a check on one of those ancestry sites?"

"Her lips parted slightly before speaking. I guess they weren't rusted shut after all. "I thought you said you couldn't find her on the Internet because her name is so common."

"That was before I had Michael's serial number."

Bonnie's eyes nearly popped out of their sockets. "You got his social security number? How'd you do that?"

Fred had gone back to sleep, but raised his head again at Bonnie's excitement, for in addition to spring-loaded eyes, she had also raised her voice several octaves.

"Not his social security number, Bon, I got his military ID number. You know, the ones they used to put on dog tags. Anyway, it should be all I need to find his family tree on one of those ancestry sites."

"Promise you won't tell him, or her, about the letter if we find him?"

Even Fred did a double take, but I'm sure it wasn't because of what she'd said. He was probably looking for a handout. "Oh, right, the bastard child," I said, and held up my right hand, "Scout's honor."

She tried to act sternly. "You were never a Boy Scout, Jake. And I'd love to take you up on lunch, but I'm having lunch with Margot."

"She's coming up here? I thought she hated the mountains."

She smiled, exposing deep laugh lines. "No, silly. I'm meeting her at that new restaurant by Colorado Mills, and then we're going shopping. The timing couldn't be better."

Once more, I imitated the stone wall between our houses and stared with my mouth open.

"The realtor, Jake. Margot knows some very important people. I'll ask her to have what's his name checked out."

"Brendon Cole. His name is Brendon Cole, Bon."

***

I hadn't bothered to tell Bonnie that I could search the Internet for Brendon faster than she could get Margot's friends to do it. I could have, but let it go, knowing it would give her something to do. Instead of searching for Brendon, I went to work looking for Michael Johnson. My search didn't take long before I realized it would have to wait. The sites that claimed to have his information wanted more than my credit card would allow.

In the end, I spent a few hours taking pictures of my motor home and posting them on Craigslist. I had no sooner finished when I got a text from Lisa asking me to meet her for lunch. She said she had some information on the witch next door that she couldn't wait to share. I assumed she was referring to Debbie's neighbor.

Chapter Eight

When Lisa didn't answer my call back, I left a message telling her Fred and I were on our way, and to either call me or text where she wanted to have lunch. There wasn't any rain in the forecast and the temperature in town was supposed to be in the sixties, so I was hoping we could meet in the park again. We no sooner turned on to I-70 when my phone rang.

"Hi, Lisa," I said without looking at the caller ID. "So tell me, how'd the witch hunt go?"

There was a long pause. "Witch hunt? Oh, Halloween. I get it now. Is that what was so important. You wanted to send me on a witch hunt?"

"Sergeant Cruz?"

"Very good, Mr. Martin. At least you didn't call me Penelope. So what's this you found on your walk board, whatever that is?"

Now it was my turn to be speechless. The image of Morticia Addams came rushing back as I remembered the detective's dark eyes watching me the last time we'd met.

"Jake? Are you still there?"

"I must have lost the signal for a minute. We just passed the Lookout Mountain exit. The signal's not that good here on the backside of the towers."

"We?"

"Me and Fred, my dog."

"Oh, I remember that beautiful dog. A golden, isn't he? And so smart, too. But I didn't call to…" Call waiting cut off her last words. A quick glance told me it was Lisa.

"Sorry about that, Sarge. Someone else was calling me at the same time. What were you saying?"

"Can you meet me at Ms. Walker's house?" Whatever friendly tone I had imagined earlier had vanished. She sounded more like I did when I answered a call from a telemarketer during a final Jeopardy question.

"Uh, sure. What time?"

"Be there by noon, and this better be good." The line went dead before I could respond.

I looked over at Fred who had listened to the entire conversation. "What do you think, old man? Are we in trouble because of your nose again?" He laid his head between his paws and looked up at me without answering.

Another quick glance at my phone before calling Lisa back told me I only had half an hour to make a forty-five-minute drive. I pressed the icon that dials the last incoming number to save time.

"The number you have dialed is not a working number. Please check the number and dial again."

"What? She just called me. How could it not be a working number?" I yelled at my phone.

Fred raised his head at the tone of my voice. He looked worried. "Didn't mean to disturb your nap," I said and pulled over so I could punch in the number manually. This time, I got her voice mail.

"Uh, we're not going to make it for lunch, Lisa. That detective wants me to meet her at your sister's house at noon, so I'm afraid I'll have to cancel any lunch plans you made. Can we do dinner instead? Call me and let me know."

***

Cruz's unmarked car was parked out front when Fred and I showed up fifteen minutes late. I knew it was her car because I hadn't seen a car with hubcaps in years. I didn't know it was even possible to buy a car without hubcaps anymore. She wasn't in the car, but the front door to Debbie's house was open, so I put Fred on his leash and went inside.

"Glad you could make it, Mr. Martin." I found her in the upstairs bedroom, looking inside one of the armoire drawers I had stacked next to the wall. She turned and made a show of looking at her watch. Then with a dismissive wave of the hand, she pointed to the stack of drawers. "I don't remember those being there."

"Must have been your forensics team," I said, hoping she didn't see through my lie. The last thing I needed right now was to bring up the letters.

She turned and stared at me, or so it seemed. Her eyes lids were so narrow I couldn't see her pupils. "Right, and I'm Mother Teresa. But petty theft isn't my department. Why don't you show me that walk board, and while you're at it, what in the Sam Hill is a walk board?"

"The boards I walk on when I'm on my scaffold. Fred found something on the bottom side of the board closest to the floor." I was about to tell her I'd already taken them home when I saw a shadow appear on the wall behind her.

Her gaze turned to the visitor. "Ms. Carpenter, your sister's contractor was just explaining to me how much smarter his dog is than my entire CSI team." Her smile couldn't have been any phonier if she had painted it on. "But I'm glad you're here. Do you know if anything is missing from those dresser drawers over there?"

"I'm a handyman, not a contractor, and it's called an armoire." The words had no sooner left my mouth than I realized the mistake I made of correcting her. She turned toward me with a sneer the real Morticia could never imitate.

Lisa must have felt the tension as well. "No, Sergeant. I believe Jake was instructed to throw everything in the dumpster, including the dress... I mean the armoire." Her smile betrayed her play on words.

Cruz looked away from Lisa and checked the watch on her wrist again. Lisa wasted no time in walking over to Fred and ruffling his fur. "Why don't you tell the nice detective what you found, Freddie?"

He barked in response, causing Sergeant Cruz to look up from her watch.

"He says he doesn't know but thought it tasted pretty good," Lisa said, laughing.

Cruz didn't return the laugh. "The board, Mr. Martin. Can I see it, please?"

"It's back at my place. When you didn't call me back, I loaded everything into my Jeep and took it home."

She took a deep breath and slowly exhaled. "Can you describe what's on it then?"

"It looked like Debbie was trying to tell us who hit her in the head. The letters JM were written in what looked to me like blood."

Lisa looked up from petting Fred. "I've been thinking about that, Jake. You don't wear Westons do you? Maybe somebody left a peanut butter and jelly sandwich on the board and you stepped on it, leaving those initials. That would explain why Fred found it. Wouldn't it?"

"Not unless they sell them at Wal-mart. I don't even know what they are."

Cruz finally smiled for real. "A very expensive line of shoes, Mr. Martin. But she has a point, may I see yours?"

She stood perfectly still holding out her hand, so I removed my right boot and gave it to her.

"EVER, I'm not sure what the next letter is, but it isn't a J or M," she said, squinting to make out the brand name. "By the looks of it, you've stepped on a lot worse things than jelly sandwiches."

Lisa and I both had to laugh.

"Except those aren't my work boots. Those are expensive hiking boots I paid all of ten dollars for at Goodwill, I'm not about to ruin them with drywall mud and paint." No one laughed at my joke. Maybe they thought I was serious.

Cruz's forced smile was back. "Then I take it your work shoes are probably not Westons either. Do me a favor, Jake. Next time you get one of your brainstorms, please leave the detective work to the professionals."

"I wasn't playing detective, Sergeant. I simply said I think Debbie wrote the initials of the guy who did her in when she was lying under my scaffold, dying. Besides, if it were my boots, the initials on the board would be MJ, with a backward J."

Both girls looked at me with wide blank eyes.

"I had a similar experience a few years back. Long story short, the impression is reversed, kind of like a printer's type." I wanted to elaborate but felt an elbow in my side.

The sergeant didn't miss Lisa poking me, and unconsciously turned my boot over and over in her hands. "I'd still like to see that walk board, Mr. Martin."

"Are you going to keep my boot, then?" I asked.

She paused long enough to remove her cell phone from inside her suit jacket, and took a picture of the sole before handing me back the boot. Then instead of putting the phone back in her pocket she pressed a few virtual buttons and read something I couldn't see before looking back up at me. "Do you still live on Columbine Circle?"

"Yes."

"And that's where we can find the walk boards?"

"Uh huh."

"Do you object to us taking a look to see if it matches the pattern on your work boots?"

"No, of course not."

She smiled condescendingly and put the phone back in her jacket. "Thank you for your cooperation, Mr. Martin. I'll have someone come by to take a look, so please don't do anything that might erase the food stains from those boards or your boots."

***

Lisa watched Sergeant Cruz pull away while I held Fred by his collar. We had followed the sergeant as far as the front porch and waited for her to leave before either of us spoke. Lisa turned around and pulled tightly on the thin jacket she was wearing before zipping it up. She didn't look happy. "You didn't need to go into detail about your shoes, Jake. Now she's probably going to keep me here until she checks out those damn shoes."

***

Bonnie's fingers barely touched as she gripped her oversized coffee cup with both hands, trying to ward off the cold evening air. The temperature was in the high sixties when Fred and I had stopped off to see if her investigation had gone any better than ours, so we all went out on her deck for coffee. Now that the sun was down, the chilly air would make a polar bear shiver. Bonnie had offered to warm us up with some of her fortified cider but settled for coffee when I declined. "She actually elbowed you to shut up in front of the detective?" she asked after I'd told her about my day.

"Yeah. I never know when to shut up. You know how I go on about nothing when I'm nervous. Sergeant Cruz had all but dismissed the message on the walk board until I opened my big mouth and then she saw Lisa try to stop me from talking."

"Why would she do that? It's like she's hiding something."

"She says she needs to get back to Kansas City by the end of the week and didn't want me to do anything that could delay her."

Bonnie rolled her eyes before speaking. "Right. She's hiding something, Jake. I know if Margot had died under mysterious circumstances, I'd want the cops to follow up on any clue they had, no matter how long it took."

"Yeah, that's what I've been thinking, too." I had unconsciously reached out for Fred to ruffle his fur, so I didn't have to look Bonnie in the eyes. "What do you think, Freddie? Did Lisa kill her sister?"

Fred cocked his head and stared at me with wide, brown eyes.

"That looks like a yes to me, Jake," Bonnie said.

I looked up in time to see a smile before she hid it with her hand. "What you two great sleuths seem to forget, Bon, is that Lisa was in Kansas City when Debbie died."

Her smile was gone. "She really got to you, didn't she?" she asked, holding both her hands together in the shape of a steeple to support her chin.

I could feel myself blush. I hadn't felt this way about another woman since Julie died, and it made me feel guilty. "I'm just saying it's physically impossible for her to have killed Debbie. And as for any feelings I might have had, she let me know in no uncertain words that whatever we had going was over when she left Fred and me standing on her porch after Cruz left."

Bonnie dropped her chin support and raised her eyebrows. "She didn't ask you in?"

"Not a word. She just went back inside and slammed the door on us. But enough of my day. Was Margot able to get any information on the realtor?"

"Did she ever."

"Well, are you going to tell me?" I asked, before taking a sip of my now cold coffee.

Bonnie nearly squealed trying to tell me what Margot found. "Debbie had just won a two hundred thousand dollar judgment against him."

"What?" I asked, raising my own eyebrows. "How'd she get that info so quickly? I spent an hour on the Internet and couldn't find anything on him I didn't have to pay for."

The corners of Bonnie's lips rose ever so slightly and her crow's feet grew deeper. "I told you, she has friends in high places."

She took a sip of her coffee before continuing. "This really needs some help, Jake."

"Okay, I'll get Jack Daniels to warm it for you, but first, tell me what Margot found out about Brendon."

Bonnie was all smiles and set her cup down on the table. "Now where was I? Oh yeah. It seems Debbie sued him for defrauding her and then turned him into the board of realtors. She not only won the suit, but it looks like he will lose his license, too."

I had started to put my cup down but now held it in midair. I must have looked like a scene from a movie that someone put on pause.

Bonnie laughed at my response, then went on. "Debbie had signed a quit claim so he could get her a loan in his name. She didn't have the credit to get a mortgage of her own. Anyway, it looks like he kept the money. She promptly sued him, but the house went into foreclosure before her case went to court. Long story short, the bank foreclosed and was trying to evict her, but she got a stay from the judge who eventually ruled in her favor."

"Does Lisa know any of this?"

"I would think so, but I guess that depends on how close they were. Margot said the judgment came a day before Debbie died, so it's possible Lisa doesn't know yet. But I really doubt it, Jake. Sisters aren't like you guys, we share everything."

"You and Margot are identical twins, so I don't doubt you know what the other is thinking. Lisa and Debbie, on the other hand, are step sisters, and from what Lisa has told me, were never close."

Bonnie shrugged and picked up her cup, felt it had become cold, and nodded toward her kitchen. I took my cue and got up to fetch her bourbon.

***

"Ah, much better," she said after I returned and she poured a huge shot into her coffee. "Now I can continue if I can remember where I was."

"You were talking about sisters sharing everything, but even if Lisa did know about the judgment, it's no reason to kill Debbie. The person who had the most to gain is obviously the realtor," I said, scratching my chin. "I wonder if he has an alibi for the day Debbie died."

Bonnie put her fortified coffee back on the table and looked at me with vacant eyes. She had gone back to supporting her head with both hands and elbows on the table. "I could call him under the pretense of wanting to sell my house."

"Mr. Cole, Could you come out and list my house? And by the way, what were you doing the day Debbie Walker died?" I said, using the closest thing to a falsetto voice I could muster.

"That's not funny, Jake." But before I could apologize, Beethoven interrupted us, and my mood changed completely when I saw who it was.

Chapter Nine

Later that night I did what little research I could on Debbie's realtor while Fred slept at my feet. How I envied dogs. I tried to remember the last time I'd slept more than four or five hours straight. I could only hope to come back as a golden retriever in my next life, but with my luck, it would be to a family in Indonesia where dogs are considered a delicacy.

The research wasn't because I doubted Bonnie or her sister. I needed something more substantial to show Sergeant Cruz. The phone call had been from Cruz telling me she would be out in the morning to examine my walk boards. That's when I had the bright idea to tell her about Debbie's realtor, once I had more than hearsay to convince her that he had a motive to murder Debbie.

Eventually, I did confirm what Margot had told Bonnie about the lawsuit. I didn't get all the details because the website wanted my credit card and a monthly subscription if I wanted the specifics, but it should be enough for Sergeant Cruz. I'm sure she has much better sources to check if I could convince her the realtor had a motive to do Debbie in.

It looked like the suit had become nasty. Debbie had won a judgment last year only to have it nullified by the bankruptcy court when Brendon filed for Chapter Seven bankruptcy. She appealed that decision claiming fraud. The appeal went in her favor, and Brendon Cole was back on the hook for a little over two hundred thousand.

It must have been around ten or so when I forgot about Mr. Cole. Someone sent me an email in response to the ad I put on Craigslist for the motor home. "Looks like we hooked a live one, Freddie. He wants to come out tomorrow to check it out. Do think you can get up before ten tomorrow?"

Fred opened his eyes and raised his head at the mention of his name. He made me feel bad for waking him.

***

Sergeant Cruz woke me Tuesday morning around nine. "Mr. Martin?" she asked after I stumbled to answer the phone. I had forgotten I'd placed it on my dresser to charge overnight, and nearly missed her call. Luckily, the dresser is in the corner of my bedroom. If the phone had been downstairs on my desk, I would have missed the call altogether.

I managed to clear my throat before answering. "Yes."

"Something's come up and I'll have to postpone my visit this morning. Are you free this afternoon?"

"I'd have to check my calendar. Can you hold a second?" Of course, I was free. The guy who wanted to check out the motor home should be long gone by then, but she didn't need to know that. I counted to thirty before speaking again. "Looks like I'll be home after two. I'm supposed to give a couple estimates this morning, but my afternoon is free. Does that work?"

"See you then," she said and disconnected.

Fred was at the door before I could end the call on my phone. He barked once before scratching it. "Okay, hold your horses, Freddie," I said, and walked over to let him out. I didn't have the heart to tell him we would be skipping breakfast at Bonnie's. I only had a couple hours to clean up the motor home before the potential buyer showed up.

He barked again before I got to the door. This time, there was a hint of urgency in his bark. Most people would never be able to tell the difference, but since I had left the city and moved into our mountain cabin, I spent more time with Fred than I did with people. He had a bark for potty time, one for when he was hungry, another when he wanted to play, and most importantly, the one he just used telling me someone, or something, was out there.

The hair along Fred's spine was standing straight up like a Mohawk, and he was growling. I couldn't open the door or he would be out chasing whatever was out there, and I couldn't take the chance it was a bear or mountain lion. I was wishing I'd put a window in my door when I grabbed him by the collar and opened it just enough to peek out to see what had him so upset.

He saw his chance, slipped out of the collar, and was out the door like a greyhound at the dog track when the gates are opened. "Fred! Get back here, now!" I might as well have yelled at the trees for what good it did.

There was a car on the road next to my shed spitting out so much dirt and gravel that I couldn't tell what it was.

Whoever it was, fled the scene when he heard Fred coming. But Fred was smarter than the intruder and ran down toward Bonnie's to try and catch him on the lower road. If Fred were to come back as a greyhound in his next life, the rabbit wouldn't stand a chance. I took off running down the hill after Fred, yelling for him to stop. Bonnie must have heard all the commotion. She was standing on her deck in her pajamas as Fred raced after the cloud of dust.

Fred came back defeated by the time I made it down to Bonnie's but continued to bark at the car that was long gone. "What were you thinking, Freddie? You could have been killed!"

He took a break from barking at the car, and looked up at me, smiling. I imagine he would have said, "I did good, huh, Dad?" if he could talk.

"What's that all about, Jake?" I hadn't seen Bonnie come down from her deck, for my back had been turned to her while I was scolding Fred. Somehow, she had found time to rush back inside and get a robe to cover her pajamas. It didn't seem to help though, for she was shivering in the cold, mountain air.

"Why don't you get dressed and drive on up, Bon? I'll tell you about it over some hot coffee."

She turned to go back into her house, stopped after a few feet and turned back to face me. "Why can't you tell me now, Jake? Was that Lisa? Did she spend the…" She paused long enough for me to know she was searching for the right word that wouldn't offend me.

"Lisa? Why on earth would you think it was her?"

Bonnie couldn't look me in the eyes. "I... Well, I assumed... I mean how many people do you know with Missouri plates?"

"The car had Missouri plates?"

"You didn't know?"

"No. I barely saw it before Fred took off. It was parked between my motor home and the shed."

Bonnie looked up quickly and grabbed my arm. "My God, Jake. Don't tell me you had another break in?" Her touch caught me off guard. She reminded me so much of how my mother had acted the time I'd been in a fight with the class bully and lost.

"We're okay, Bon. He was parked by my shed, but Fred scared him off before he had a chance to break in. At least I think that's what happened. I need to get back up there and check it out."

She leaned in closer, running her tongue over her lips. "Promise me you'll wait until I get there. It won't take me long to get dressed, and I keep Greg's old revolver in the closet. I'll bring it just in case."

I had already started back up the hill but stopped at the mention of the gun. She had told me stories about how Greg won several quick-draw trophies in his younger days. If that was the gun she meant, I doubted if she knew how to use it. They were single-action revolvers that required the shooter to cock the hammer manually for each shot.

"He's gone, Bon. You won't need Greg's old gun, but you may want to bring Jack Daniels to warm your coffee."

***

Fred and I didn't wait for Bonnie. We went straight to my shed once we'd climbed the hill up to my cabin. I went over and checked the padlock; it hadn't been broken or smashed. Fred took it upon himself to check out my scaffold and pile of two by twelves I used for walk boards. I was still testing the lock when he barked.

I went over to see what he found. "What's up, Freddie? Chatter making a nest for the winter?" Chatter was the name Bonnie had given a local squirrel Fred couldn't catch.

He looked at me to make sure he had my attention then pointed at the boards with his nose. All of a sudden I felt like someone had punched me in the chest, I knew without looking at it, that the writing on the walk board would be destroyed. There was a can of spray paint lying on the ground next to the boards.

I went over and checked anyway. Debbie's message, or what I thought had been a message, was covered in red paint. I bent over to rub Fred's head and pick up the can of paint when I heard a car pull into my driveway. I couldn't see who it was because my motor home blocked the view. When I felt the muscles in Fred's back stiffen, I knew it wasn't Bonnie, so I assumed it was the guy who wanted to see my motor home.

***

The vehicle parked in my driveway wasn't a car. It was a decked out Hummer with huge wheels and darkly-tinted windows. The wheels had some kind of fancy hubcaps or spinners that continued to spin long after the beast had come to a stop. My ex would have called it a pimp mobile. I approached the Hummer holding Fred with one hand and the spray can with the other. I held him by the nape of his neck because his collar was still in my cabin where I'd left it after he'd slipped out of it. I knew he wouldn't hurt the guy, but I wasn't so sure about strangers hurting Fred. I nearly let him go when I saw who got out of the car.

"Nice wheels, Sergeant. That must have set your department back a pretty penny."

She didn't smile or look at me. She peeked over the sunglasses she was wearing, looking at the paint can. "Don't worry, Mr. Martin. It didn't raise your taxes. Not even an ugly penny. It was confiscated during a drug bust. I knew I'd need four-wheel drive up here. My sedan would be destroyed on these roads."

This wasn't going well. I needed to get her on my side before telling her about the walk board. "I didn't mean to get you riled up, Sarge. Just making small talk."

She raised her left hand, pointing at the spray paint. "Would you mind putting that down? And it's Sergeant Cruz. I'm not a marine."

"It's just paint, Sergeant Cruz," I said but threw it aside anyway. "I didn't expect to see you so early. I thought we had a two o'clock appointment."

"And I thought you had some estimates to give this morning." She pushed her glasses to the tip of her nose with her right index finger and stared straight into my eyes. She couldn't be more than five eight to my six two, but she made me feel small.

I was rescued from coming up with a smart answer when Bonnie came racing into my drive and parked behind the Sergeant's pimp mobile. We both turned to look. Fred broke loose of my grip and ran past the Sergeant to greet Bonnie, with his tail wagging like he hadn't seen her in a week.

Bonnie was out of her Cherokee and heading toward us when Fred ran up to her. She bent down to pet him. "Hello, Freddie. Did you miss me already?"

Cruz removed her sunglasses and smiled for the first time since she'd arrived.

I welcomed the opportunity to change the subject. "Sergeant, I'd like you to meet a good friend and neighbor of mine, Bonnie Jones."

Bonnie stood up slowly, bracing her back with her right forehand before walking over to us. "Glad to meet you, Sergeant. Jake has told me so much about you," she said, extending her hand.

"Oh?" she said, raising her eyebrows. "Has he now?"

I cut in before Bonnie repeated something I'd said, and shouldn't have. "About your work on the case. I was telling her how you thought Debbie's death was an accident, and not due to foul play."

Bonnie wasn't listening. Her eyes were focused on Sergeant Cruz's left hand. I had already noticed the lack of a wedding band, so I prayed Bonnie didn't get any ideas about matchmaking. "That's because he's a mystery writer. And a pretty good one, if you ask me. He may not have a lot right now, but wait until some New York publisher discovers him. He'd be a great catch, he would."

"I'm sure the Sergeant didn't come here to hear about my writing, Bon. Did you, Sergeant?" I could only hope Cruz hadn't followed Bonnie's train of thought. I knew she had jumped the track and was saying I'd be a good husband, but with luck, the Sergeant would think she meant a great catch for the publisher.

Cruz laughed, then bit her lip to hide her smile. "No, I didn't, Mr. Martin. Though I'd love to hear more, I need to see that walk board with the message you told me about."

Chapter Ten

Fred beat us to the pile of two by twelves stacked between my motor home and shed. I could tell from the happy grin on his face how proud he was to have discovered the message which was giving him so much attention. Cruz went straight to him and bent down to ruffle his fur. "Do you want to show me which board your master squashed his lunch on, Freddie?" she asked, smiling.

Fred got up and went over to the freshly painted board, then turned back looking for her admiration as if he understood what she'd said.

Cruz unzipped her jacket to get to her smartphone from an inside pocket. I couldn't help but notice the holster attached to her belt with what looked like a small caliber automatic. She went over to the walk board, ready to take a picture, and froze. Then without taking a picture, put the phone in her left hand and reached out to touch the fresh paint with her right index finger. It looked like she was about to taste it, but looked over at me instead.

"I tried to tell you earlier, Sergeant, when you told me to drop the paint can."

"Well, tell me now, Jake, and it better be good. Why did you paint over the message?"

Jake? Whatever happened to Mr. Martin, I thought.

Bonnie answered before I could. "It was the guy from Missouri. Wasn't it, Jake?"

"Missouri?" Cruz asked.

"Somebody driving a car with Missouri plates painted over the message less than half an hour ago. I'm surprised he didn't run into you on the way down to Upper Bear." I managed to answer before Bonnie.

Cruz fished out a tissue from one of her pockets and wiped her finger while processing what we'd said. "I did pass a minivan with Missouri plates coming up the road."

"That sounds like Lisa's van, but Bonnie said she saw a man driving it."

"I think it was a man, Jake. You can't be too sure nowadays. It could have been Lisa disguised as a man." Bonnie was nearly jumping up and down. Most people would think she had to pee, but I knew better. She tended to get excited when it looked like we might be on the way to solving another murder.

Cruz looked blankly at Bonnie without saying a thing. I wondered if that's how the Spanish inquisitors looked before deciding to burn a heretic at the stake. Then she turned toward me with the same look. That's when I remembered my history teacher telling us how the accused could have his throat garroted if he repented before being burned. "Let me get this straight. You two are telling me that someone painted over the evidence before I got here, and you think that someone is Lisa Carpenter?"

"It's starting to look that way," I answered.

"Who else could it be?" Bonnie was no longer jumping up and down. Either she had wet her Depends or read my mind about the garrote. "Jake told me she was really upset when he told you about the message. I'll bet anything she killed her sister and tried to make it look like an accident."

Cruz seemed to consider what Bonnie said before turning toward me again. "I'll have someone from the lab come and get that board, Mr. Martin. We have ways of seeing under the paint, so I'll ask you again not to tamper with it anymore."

"No problem, Sergeant. I'll even lock it in my shed this time…if that's okay."

She paused long enough to take a deep breath before slowly exhaling. "Yes, but I hope for your sake the shed doesn't get broken into or burn to the ground. Oh, and I'll take that can of spray paint with me if you don't object."

"Not at all. But don't get caught writing graffiti in the ladies' restroom. My prints are all over it."

She didn't look amused, so I tried to be more serious. "My prints are in the national database. Any others you find will be the perp who painted the board. And I'll put Fred on guard duty until your lab boys get here."

Fred had been sitting like a stone statue at my side. He looked up and barked when he heard his name.

The Sergeant finally smiled before reaching down to pat him on the head. "It looks like you're the only thing keeping your master out of jail, big boy. I hope you don't let him down."

***

"I think she likes you, Jake," Bonnie said after taking a sip of her reinforced cider to ward off the morning chill. We were sitting at her deck table, discussing Sergeant Cruz, after Bonnie had talked me into a late breakfast when I got a text message from the guy who was supposed to look at my motor home. He said he couldn't make it and would reschedule. Actually, it was Fred she had conned by asking him if he was hungry. When his eyes lit up, and his tail started wagging his entire rear end at the thought of food, I didn't have the heart to refuse.

"I think she'd like to see me in handcuffs." No sooner had I said it when I realized how it sounded.

Either she didn't notice, or was too embarrassed to respond and changed the subject. "Do you really think it was Lisa? I thought we decided it must be the realtor because of the lawsuit he lost."

I had finished my breakfast, so I gave my leftovers to Fred before answering. "I'm not sure what I think anymore. No doubt the realtor has the best motive, but a minivan with Missouri plates is too much of a coincidence. I mean, how many cars do you think match that description?" I asked, while unconsciously tapping my index finger on the table. It was a habit that helped me think.

"Probably a few thousand," Bonnie answered, trying not to laugh.

"You know what I mean, Bon."

"Yes, I know, but you look so serious. Besides, how often do I get a chance to correct you?" she said, reaching over to stop my hand from tapping.

"Probably a few thousand."

"Funny, Jake," she said and stood to pick up my plate, which was now Fred's. "What a good boy you are, Freddie, saving me from having to wash your master's plate. There's not a spot on it."

Fred didn't get the pun and simply wagged his tail.

"Let me help you with those, Bon," I said, getting up from my chair.

"I've got 'em, Jake. Why don't you..." My cell phone cut her off before she could finish.

***

Bonnie was back with fresh coffee for me and more cider for herself by the time I finished my conversation. She took her seat across from me at the table, holding her cup with both hands, and looked at me with big, blue-gray eyes. "Was that who I think it was?"

"I'd ask who you thought it was, but I noticed you didn't close your door, and since your hearing is second only to Fred's..." I waited a few seconds to build a little suspense. "Yes, it was Debbie's realtor."

"Are you going to tell me what he wanted before I pee my pants?"

Chapter Eleven

I was more worried that Bonnie would have a heart attack than wet her pants, so I decided to tell her without any more theatrics. "He says Debbie's death was no accident and says her boyfriend, Ryan Best, did it."

Bonnie's right leg began to vibrate. I couldn't see it, but could feel the table shake. "What? You're not buying any of that, are you? I think he's trying to blow smoke up your butt, Jake. He killed her to get out of paying her."

The vibration suddenly stopped. "But what was that I heard about a thousand dollars?"

"He heard about the murders we solved last year and wants to hire us to prove that Ryan did it."

Bonnie was about to take a drink of her cider, but paused, holding the cup in midair. "Us? He wants to pay me, too?" Sunlight bounced off her wedding band onto Fred, making him raise a paw to shield his eyes. Any other time she would have noticed, but not this time.

"And that's just a retainer. Said he'd give us another thousand if we can nail the perp. His words, not mine," I said, reaching down to scratch Fred's head.

"Fred should have been a cat," Bonnie said. "Kitty used to push herself against me the same way he does."

The shock of being paid must have passed, or so I thought. "Is that a thousand each?"

"I didn't ask, but you already knew that."

She raised the cup to her lips and took a long sip. "I wasn't eavesdropping, Jake. It's not my fault sound travels the way it does in this chilly air."

"Sorry, Bon. I didn't mean it the way it sounded."

"Well, I'm glad you didn't turn him down. I could really use a little extra right now."

I didn't mention she wasn't alone in that category.

"I wonder why Sergeant Cruz changed her mind?" she asked.

I had to blink a few times before I got the connection. "That she thinks it's murder and not an accident?"

"Of course. What did you think I thought she thought?"

"Are you trying to give me a brain fart, Bon?"

She tilted her head the way Fred had. If I didn't know better I'd have thought she wanted me to pat her on the head, too. "She left here less than two hours ago," I said. "There is no way she could have stopped to interrogate him, and until a few hours ago she was convinced it was an accident. It doesn't smell right."

"You're not going to turn down the money, Jake. Please don't do that."

"You're assuming he has the money to pay us. Are you forgetting he filed for bankruptcy recently and he still owes two hundred thousand to whoever gets Debbie's estate?"

"That would be your girlfriend, Lisa. Wouldn't it?"

"She's not my girlfriend, Bon. I'll admit I kind of liked her, but she's a little too emotional for me."

Her foot tapping started in again. "Well, he hasn't paid her yet, so we should get the money while we can."

"Whether he has it or not is a minor issue. There's one major obstacle still in our way."

"Which is?"

"We're not licensed to do PI work, Bon. We could get into big trouble taking his money."

Her tapping stopped. She leaned back in her chair, crossing her arms, and with a huge smirk on her face, answered. "Not anymore, silly. Colorado dropped that requirement when you were in kindergarten. I guess you were too young to remember."

"Or care," I said.

Bonnie ignored my remark and went on with the history lesson. "We were the first to license PIs but dropped it in seventy-seven because it was ruled unconstitutional. I think I read somewhere that they started licensing again a few years ago, but now it's voluntary."

"How do you know all this, Bon. I know you used to teach school, but that's not the kind of subject they teach in middle school."

"Junior High…They called it Junior High, back then."

"I stand corrected."

"I took some creative writing classes at a JC. It was a night class for people who wanted to write mystery novels."

"Really? How come you never mentioned it before?"

Bonnie turned her head, looking off toward Mount Evans. "I don't know, Jake. I didn't have what it takes and it was more to save my sanity than anything else. After Dianne died…"

This conversation was going the wrong way. Bonnie was close to tears. Her daughter had died in a hit and run accident over twenty-five years ago and she never got over it. "Tell you what, Bon Bon," I said in the cheeriest voice I could muster. "How about I call him back and tell him we'll meet tomorrow and he can give us the retainer then?"

It seemed to work. Her eyes had turned red, but she was able to manage a smile.

***

Brendon Cole agreed to meet us at my cabin on Wednesday morning when I told him I couldn't make it into town for a few days. It was none of his business that I expected the lab boys to retrieve my walk board in the afternoon, so I told him I was in the middle of a manuscript rewrite for my editor. He also didn't need to know my manuscript was no more than a few scribbled notes. But he did seem eager to meet us, and when he reiterated he'd be glad to give us a retainer, I suggested he come up to my cabin first thing in the morning.

Bonnie was making small talk as we sat on my deck, drinking coffee, and waiting for Brendon. We had just finished breakfast. It was the first time I'd seen her wear makeup in ages. She had chosen to highlight her cloudy blue eyes with a darker blue liner and had some kind of foundation that hid most of her wrinkles. She even had on a dress I hadn't seen since the time she'd talked me into going to her church. It made me wonder if she was trying to dress as Ms. Marple. If she was, I'd blown it for her with my blue jeans and a long sleeve, wool shirt, for I doubt if Ms. Marple had any lumberjacks in her family.

Bonnie picked up her plate from the deck after Fred had cleaned it for her. "I don't think I've ever had pigs in a blanket made with toaster waffles. Honey instead of syrup was a nice touch, too. Is this your own recipe, Jake?"

"Just some leftovers I threw together. I haven't had a chance to run to the store, and if Brendon doesn't show up pretty soon we'll be eating squirrel." I expected that would get Fred's attention, but he was too intent on waiting to see if Bonnie had anything else she didn't want to eat.

Bonnie smiled, then slid her chair away from my little table. I didn't need to worry she'd tip over because her chair was up against the rail. "Have you given much thought on how we can prove the realtor did it?"

Fred turned and cocked his head before I could answer. We both knew what it meant--he heard something we hadn't. "Not really," I answered, looking toward the road.

"Well, you better think of something fast, Jake. I think he's here." We must have looked like those cows one sees standing by the farmer's fence watching the cars go by. All three of us were at the deck rail, faced in the direction of the road, waiting and listening.

"Not unless he's driving a police van," I said, and got up to meet the lab technicians with Fred at my heels. Bonnie said she'd join us as soon as she fixed her makeup.

***

There were two people I could see: a driver and passenger. By the way the driver was waving his hands when he spoke to his passenger, it looked like they might be arguing. Or maybe he was trying to unhook himself from his seat belt and couldn't find the latch. The guy was huge. Not big like a linebacker, but more like the fat man at a carnival.

The driver finally freed himself and stepped out of the van. I watched as the van seemed to lift itself up several inches. He didn't look happy, nor did he take his eyes off Fred when he spoke to me. "They didn't tell me we needed four-wheel drive. Christ, I'll be lucky I don't lose a muffler or something." He didn't wait for me to respond and turned back to his open cab to retrieve a clipboard before slamming the door shut.

"What a beautiful view you have." The Grinch's passenger had come around from the far side of the van. I turned in time to see her bouncing on the tips of her toes in the middle of stretching her arms. "And what a beautiful golden," she said, kneeling down to pet Fred.

The big ham gave her his best grin in response.

"Don't mind Danny," she said, looking up while giving Fred an ear rub. "He got up on the wrong side of the bed...again."

Danny scowled at her remark, glanced at his clipboard, then turned toward me. He didn't seem to be worried about my fierce dog anymore. "Are you Jake Martin?"

"Depends on who's asking," I said.

Danny rolled his eyes and reached into his jumpsuit pocket then showed me an official looking badge. "Daniel Craig, Senior Crime Scene Technician for the Jefferson County Regional Crime Laboratory."

"You don't look like James Bond." Bonnie had joined us in time to hear Danny's full name. She wore a grin wider than Fred's.

Danny glanced at his clipboard before answering. "And you, ma'am, must be Bonnie Jones?"

I silently prayed she didn't say it depends on who's asking.

"Yes, I am. But please, sir, please don't arrest him. He didn't mean to waste the time of such an important civil servant," Bonnie answered with trembling lips. Then she grabbed my arm as if to protect me. "His name is Jake Martin. And this," she said turning toward Fred, "is his very own CSI technician, Fred. Show Senior Technician Craig your badge, I mean tags, Fred."

I had to put a hand over my mouth so I didn't laugh. Danny's partner had no such qualms and nearly fell over laughing. "Sorry, Danny," she said, between laughs. "But with the mood you've been in since leaving Lakewood, you've got to admit, you had it coming."

Red-faced, but stiffer than ever, he turned toward me. "Can you show me the walk board, Mr. Martin?"

I pointed toward my shed. "Sure. It's right over there all locked away and waiting for you,"

Danny grunted his acknowledgment and started walking toward the shed without me. Actually, it was more of a waddle. I'm not saying he was obese, but he would have to be at least eight feet tall in order for his height/weight ratio to be meet federal guidelines. It didn't take me more than a few seconds to pass him and get to the shed first. Fred stayed behind at the van with the girls. He was more interested in the other technician than coming with us. He had even found an old ball from somewhere and had her playing catch.

"I can't get that damn thing in my van. What the hell was she thinking, sending us up here?" Danny said after I opened the shed door.

I could tell from his tone that it wasn't a question--not that I would have answered anyway. All I wanted now was to give him the board so he'd leave. "Let me cut off the piece you need," I answered, reaching for a battery-powered circular saw. "I'll cut off the part where the message has been covered in paint. Or, if you prefer, I'll cut it up into manageable pieces so it will fit in your van."

"Just the part with the message. If there were any prints on the rest of it, they're gone now. What the hell did you do to that board? It looks like it's been through a flood."

I didn't bother to answer and returned his dirty look with one of my own before cutting the last two feet off the board. Halfway through the cut, my battery went dead. "Damn, why is it these batteries always die when you need them the most?"

He finally cracked a smile. Not a friendly smile. More like something Freddie Kruger might make right before he cut off your head. "There's one in my van. Go ask Carly to fetch it for you," he said, then sat his fat butt on a bench and fished out a pack of cigarettes from his shirt pocket. I didn't bother to tell him the reason the bench was outside my shed was because the legs were loose. It was one of those fix-it projects on my list that I never seemed to have time to get to.

"What the..." He didn't have time to swear again before the legs gave way and he found himself sitting on the ground.

Once again, I had to choke off my laughter with my hand. "No need to borrow yours. I have another saw in my shed," I said after I recovered, acting like nothing had happened, and stepped over him to fetch my handsaw.

***

Fred was the only one who was sad to see the van leave. "You could have gone with her, traitor," I said as we watched the van bottom out on a pothole.

"I hope the jerk lost a muffler," Bonnie said.

"Be my luck they'd send me the bill," I said, bending down to take Fred's slimy tennis ball and throw it down the road. He struck out after it faster than a snake on a mouse.

Bonnie and I watched him chase the ball. The van had already passed the first bend in the road and was out of sight, so I was surprised when he stopped chasing after the ball and did his imitation of an Irish setter. He didn't know how to point, but he didn't have to.

"Are they coming back?" Bonnie asked. We both heard the sound of a vehicle scraping bottom.

I didn't have to answer once we saw a classic Dodge Charger come slowly toward us.

Chapter Twelve

I knew immediately who the forty-something guy getting out of the Charger had to be. "Looks like Brendon's here, Bon."

"Brendon?"

"Debbie's realtor, Brendon Cole."

"How can you be so sure?"

"He's wearing a Rolex. Who else could afford a watch like that?"

"Didn't you say Debbie gave one to her boyfriend?"

"That was a Tag Heuer Chronograph. I'd have never known it from a Timex until Debbie showed me before..." I stopped talking when Brendon got close enough to hear.

"Jake?" His smile was as phony as the suit he wore. I wasn't a total country bumpkin. There was a time I was an in-demand consultant to Fortune 500 companies and I had to wear the real thing. I still had them hanging in my closet, enclosed in plastic dry cleaner bags. They weren't Louis Vuittons or Armanis, but they weren't off the rack from JC Penny's like Brendon's, either. It made we wonder if his watch came from China, too. I was surprised he didn't have

Richard Houston

a couple gold teeth to go with the necklace hanging down the front of his silk shirt. "And this lovely lady must be your partner, Bonnie Jones." He held out a hand for her to shake that had more gold on it than a three-time NFL champion.

Bonnie's eyes lit up when she saw his rings and returned the handshake. "And this is the third member of our team, Fred," she said when Fred came back with his tennis ball. He ignored Brendon and dropped the ball at my feet, waiting for me to resume the game. I picked up the slimy ball and threw it as far as I could, hoping he'd be gone awhile.

Brendon saw me wipe my hand on my jeans and didn't offer his hand for me to shake. "I hope I didn't come at a bad time," he said. "A CSI van nearly ran me off the road on the way up. Was it here?"

"They just left with the walk board," Bonnie said.

"Walk board?" Brendon asked, unwrapping a butterscotch candy and throwing the wrapper on the ground.

Bonnie hesitated before answering. "The one that supposedly hit Debbie on the head and put out her lights." I didn't bother to correct her.

"Oh, I didn't know that's what they were called. What did the CSI boys want with it?" he asked, before popping the candy in his mouth.

"I think it will prove Debbie was murdered," I answered. "She wrote something on it before she died."

"But somebody sprayed paint over the message," Bonnie said. "Someone driving a minivan with Missouri plates, and I think I know who."

98

Fred's ball had rolled down the hill into a small pile of rocks. I could see him searching for it, and knew I only had a few minutes before he came back. "How about we all go on my back deck and you can tell me why you think Ryan killed Debbie? I think the coffee's still hot."

***

"It looks like I should have worn my Norrona," Brendon said with a shiver. He was standing next to my pellet stove, rubbing his hands together. His thin, knockoff suit wasn't made for October afternoons at our altitude. The deck had been out of the question once a cloud covered the sun and a west wind brought in colder air from an early snowfall on Mount Evans. Even Fred, who still had his summer coat, wanted in. He settled in at my feet, curling himself into a ball.

Bonnie and I both stared at Brendon, wondering what he meant.

"My ski jacket," he said.

"Oh," Bonnie said, rolling her eyes so I could see. "Well, I hope we're not in for an early winter."

"So, tell me why you think Debbie's boyfriend killed her." I'd had enough of the small talk and wanted to get to the point. Brendon's phony attitude reminded me too much of a used car salesman.

"I get the feeling you don't trust me, Jake?"

Bonnie nearly spit out her coffee.

"To be honest, Brendon, when it comes to motives, yours out trumps Ryan's."

"Jake! At least hear him out." Her outburst woke Fred and made him raise his head from his self-made cocoon.

"It's okay, ma'am. I know how it must look. That lawsuit she had against me does make it look like I had the motive to do her in, but believe me, it's not how it looks at first glance. I take it that's what you're referring to, Jake?"

"Yes. We wouldn't be very good investigators if we hadn't checked you out after getting your call to hire us."

"No, you wouldn't. And I'm glad you did. It only supports my hunch that you two are the right choice..." He stopped long enough to look over at Fred who was now listening like a student at a college lecture. "Or should I say, you three?"

He continued before we could answer. "Yes, she won a huge judgment against me. I suppose it could be considered a motive to kill her, but even with her dead I still have to pay, so what's the point?"

"How do you pay a dead person?" Bonnie asked.

"I have to pay her estate. And guess who gets it all?"

"Her boyfriend, Ryan Best," I said.

Brendon smiled like he'd just sold me a Yugo.

"So that's why you think he did it?" Bonnie said. "He knew she had a will and he'd get the money once she was out of the way."

Brendon's smile grew bigger as he shook his head up and down. "Well, I can see there's no shortage of brain power with this team. That's exactly what I think."

Bonnie blushed. "Jake's the smart one, but I do have an idea once in a while."

I rolled my eyes and wondered where I left my shovel--it was getting deep in here. "Which is the real reason you want to hire us, isn't it?"

"Am I that obvious?" He was no longer smiling.

Bonnie looked confused.

"If Ryan is convicted of murder, Brendon won't have to pay," I said.

Brendon smiled. "Or at the very least, prove he forged the will. He already has two felonies; the third should put him away for good."

Fred decided to make himself known and barked. Everyone looked over at him, so he barked again.

He wasn't agreeing with what I'd said. He wanted to be let out. "Guess he's had enough," I said, opening the door. A cold blast of air hit me as I watched him run toward his favorite tree.

Bonnie must have felt it too. "Looks like we might be in for a little snow tonight," she said.

"That's what the weatherman said on the way up here." Brendon was pulling the lapels of his suit jacket tight across his chest after taking out his checkbook from an inside pocket. He left his spot at the pellet stove, took a chair at my table and started writing. "That's Martin, with an I?"

I followed his lead and took the chair opposite him, next to Bonnie. "Yes, and Jacob instead of Jake."

"And mine is Bonnie Jones, like in keeping up with the Joneses."

"Ah, right. I did say one thousand each, didn't I?"

He quickly wrote out the checks and handed them to us along with his card. "I wrote Ryan's last known address on the back."

I reached for the card, but he held tight. "Just a suggestion. You might check what kind of car he drives," he said before letting go.

"I already thought of that, but the minivan had Missouri plates."

"He could have stolen it."

"Or borrowed it." Bonnie had joined us to collect her check.

Brendon took a few seconds to process her remark. "Yes, I suppose it could be anyone, but he certainly has the motive."

Bonnie and I both looked over our checks as he pulled his lapels tighter.

"I have a friend with the DMV who can tell us what cars Ryan has registered," I said, rising from my chair to let him know the meeting was over. "We'll let you know what we find."

I followed Brendon out while Bonnie stayed inside cleaning the kitchen table. He was halfway down my front stairs when Fred came back with his ball. I quickly cut between them, took the ball from Fred before he could force it into Brendon's hands, and threw it down the hill. "I think you're good to go now," I said, not bothering to offer a handshake.

***

"Do you still have connections with the DMV, Jake?" Bonnie and I were back at my kitchen table, trying to decide what to do next. Fred had opted for his bed next to the pellet stove.

"No, that was Julie's friend who worked there. I just said that to make it sound like we knew what we were doing. But I suppose it wouldn't hurt to ask her. She took me aside after the funeral and said to call her if I needed anything."

Bonnie got up and went over to the sink. "People say those things at funerals. I don't think they really mean them."

"No, I suppose not." I watched her proceed to rinse out the coffee pot, wondering if she was going to do my dishes or make more coffee. Sometimes I wondered if I had become her adopted son. My curiosity was sated when I saw her reach into the cupboard. "You read my mind, Bon. I was going to ask if you wanted more coffee."

"I'm not sure it would help, anyway," she said.

"Why's that? Coffee always helps me."

She let out a short laugh and tapped the side of her head. "There I go again. Not the coffee. I mean I doubt if Julie's friend could trace the plates. They're from Missouri, remember?"

It was my turn to laugh. "I don't think that would be a problem. I remember reading something about a government mandate called the Real ID that forces states to share their data. Not that they couldn't do it before, if the truth was known."

She joined me at the table after starting my coffee maker. "You and your conspiracy theories. Next thing I know you'll be telling me they know what I had for breakfast."

I held a finger to my lips. "Shh, they may be listening."

"Whatever, Jake. But those plates still point back to Lisa. I know you've got the hots for her and don't want to think about it, but I'll bet anything it was her."

"She was kind of cute, and she did like Fred, so, yeah, I liked her a little."

"Well, get over it lover boy. Start thinking with your brain. Why would she try to destroy murder evidence?"

"You think she did it?"

"Duh."

"Someone could have borrowed her car." I put the emphasis on borrow. "If anything, I think we need to at least ask her."

Bonnie cocked her head and let her eyes stare at the wall before answering. "I suppose that's possible. I hadn't thought about her boyfriend borrowing it."

"She has a boyfriend?"

"Not her, silly, Debbie. I'll bet it's that Ryan Best and the message he destroyed is about him."

"If Fred didn't destroy it first."

Bonnie looked over at Fred. "You wouldn't do that, would you, Freddie?" His legs were moving and his eyes darting back and forth under closed lids. He didn't answer and kept on dreaming.

The coffee machine beeped to let me know it was done. "So, are you buying Brendon's story?" I asked, getting up to refill our cups.

"Aren't you?"

"Maybe. The jury's out on that decision until I can check it out."

She looked at me blankly when I put her cup on the table in front of her.

"The story about Ryan getting it all, Bon. Until we can verify the facts, that's all it is – a story."

"But if it wasn't him, then who?"

"I wish I knew. Who has a motive to kill?"

"Two hundred thousand sounds like a good motive to me."

"Yes, but is it really Ryan who stands to inherit everything Debbie had, or is that all a smoke screen created by Brendon? If there isn't a will, wouldn't Lisa be the one to inherit? And then there's the letter."

Bonnie raised an eyebrow and stared at me. I'm sure if her head had been made of glass, I would have seen gears turning. "I forgot about the letter, Jake. Do you think someone would really kill over that?"

"Possibly," I answered. "Like I said before, if the illegitimate child is someone important who would be ruined by the revelation...but this is the twenty-first century. Maybe a hundred years ago it would have made a difference in an election or high office, but not now. In fact, it would probably help win whatever office the person was seeking.

No, I say follow the money. Greed is the number one motive for murder."

"Next to a jilted lover," Bonnie said.

"Then that leaves out the letter. Unless the lover is a zombie. That love affair is over seventy years old. But you do have a point, Bon. Maybe it was Ryan. Not because of any inheritance. Maybe Debbie was going to dump him?"

Bonnie's eyes grew wider. "Or he was going to dump her--for her sister."

"Back to Lisa, are we?"

"Men! Can't you see she was using you? If she really cared, why hasn't she returned any of your calls?"

She had me there. Lisa could have me arrested for stalking with all the text messages I'd sent her. "But she was in Kansas City when Debbie died. She didn't even know Ryan until she came out here."

Bonnie put her empty cup down on the table a little too hard. "How do you know that, Jake? Because she told you?"

"All right, Bon. Don't shoot the messenger. I'll put her on the list, too. In the meantime, we need to come up with a plan. When I was a consultant, I would have been shown the door if I didn't have a project plan on what I was going to do for the customer, and how I was going to do it."

Bonnie walked over to my kitchen counter, opened my junk drawer, and returned to the table with a notepad. She knew my kitchen better than I, for I didn't remember putting the pad in there. "Okay, boss, what's our plan?" she said, holding a pen millimeters above the pad like a kid ready to start taking her SATs.

"Let's start with a list of suspects, their motive for killing Debbie, and their alibis."

Bonnie laid down her pen. "That's not a plan, Jake."

"I'm getting to that, Bon. Once we know who to investigate we can decide how to go about it."

She picked up her pen and started writing. "Okay. Number one on the list is Ryan. His motive is money because Debbie left him everything."

"And number two is Brendon," I said. "With Debbie and Ryan out of the way, he gets to keep his two hundred thousand--or so he thinks."

She stopped writing and looked up at me. "What does that mean, or so he thinks?"

"Are you forgetting Lisa, the next of kin? I think she would be the next in line to inherit the estate."

"Then she's next on our list, for all the reasons you mention. Anyone else, Jake?"

"Well, there's the crazy neighbor. Crazy doesn't need a motive. Anything could have ticked her off to pick up a hammer or something and hit Debbie over the head."

She wrote as fast as her fingers would move and finished with a huge grin. "See, Jake, I told you we made a great team. Maybe we should open our own detective agency when this is over. We could call it the Jones and Martin Agency."

Fred woke from his nap and went over to Bonnie to see why she was so excited. His ears were laid back and his tail was down. She took one look at him and laughed. "I'm sorry, Fred. Make that Jones, Martin and Fred Agency. Or do you want top billing?" Fred gave out a short bark, and we both laughed.

"Okay, Bon. I think our list of suspects is good enough. If anyone else pops up during the investigation, we can add them to the list. Let's get on with our plan."

Her pen went back to the pad and she looked up at me in anticipation.

I hesitated, for I didn't have a clue what to say.

"Well," she said. "I'm waiting."

"Maybe we're in over our heads, Bon."

"You don't know what to do, do you, Jake?"

"It's not exactly like writing a program. That was a piece of cake compared to this."

Bonnie set her pen down and picked up the check Brendon had given her. "Okay, Sherlock. Then if you don't mind Watson making a suggestion, shouldn't we at least attempt to earn our money?"

"So you think we should start with Ryan?"

She smiled. "Maybe Sergeant Cruz can run that DMV check for you."

"And just how do I get her to do that? Besides, it's a complete waste of time, anyway. We already know the minivan belongs to Lisa. The odds of Ryan owning a similar van with Missouri plates is astronomical," I said then, reached down to pet Fred; it always helped me to think more clearly.

"No, Bon," I said looking back up at her. "There's got to be more to it."

Bonnie looked puzzled. "To what, Jake?"

"Running that DMV check. Brendon's not stupid. Surely he realizes the minivan belongs to Lisa. I think he has other reasons for having us run that check. I mean, think about it, Bon. Anyone can run those checks for a lot less than what he's paying us. The only reason I can think of why he wants us to do it is because he wants us to find out something about Ryan that he already knows. Something he can't tell us, or doesn't want to."

"Sort of like telling a kid something, huh Jake? If you let them think it's their idea, then they're more likely to believe it."

"Exactly."

"All the more reason you should do it, or get Sergeant Cruz to do it for you."

"Yes, but not Cruz. I'll pay the fee to one of those online databases and get a complete background check on Ryan. Then..." I was interrupted by Beethoven's fifth on my cell phone. One look at the message, and I could feel the blood drain from my face.

"Who is it, Jake?" Bonnie asked.

"Cruz, Bon. It's Sergeant Cruz."

Chapter Thirteen

Sergeant Cruz turned a few heads as she walked toward me. She had chosen a dark suit that matched her eyes perfectly. "Nice to see you again, Jake," she said, taking a seat opposite me. Sure it is, I thought. I'm sure she wanted to see me again as much as a kid selling magazines door-to-door.

"Me too," I answered, trying not to stare. "I mean, I'm glad to see you too, not me." She had done something with her hair to make her look like a cover girl from one of those magazines I see at the checkout lanes all the time. She was absolutely gorgeous.

She smiled and picked up a menu. "And Ms. Jones? I take it she couldn't make it?"

"Bonnie wanted to come, but she got a call from her sister saying she didn't feel well and needed a ride to the doctor's."

"I almost expected you to sneak your dog, what's his name, in here as a service dog. I thought you two were inseparable." She wasn't looking at the menu when she spoke. She was focused on me.

"Fred's in my Jeep. And before you think of arresting me for animal cruelty, it's a scathing fifty degrees and cloudy out there. Besides, all the windows are open a crack."

Cruz put the menu aside and sat back in her seat. "All these pictures are making me hungry. I wish I had time to order something besides coffee. So if you don't mind, let's cut the small talk, and tell me what you know about Ryan Best."

"So it was him in the minivan. How did you find out?"

"I didn't say that, Jake."

"But I'm right, aren't I?"

She looked away briefly, trying to flag down our waitress, then turned her attention back to me. "Let's get back to my question, Jake. Do you know anyone who might want to hurt Ryan? And please don't answer with another question."

I had to think quickly. I didn't want to tell her about Brendon hiring Bonnie and me to get something on Ryan, but I didn't want to lie to her either. Luckily, our waitress saw Cruz and came over, giving me time to think.

"Have you decided on something?" she asked the sergeant.

"Yes. I think I'll have something to eat after all."

Cruz didn't skip a beat. Once the waitress was gone she looked me straight in the eyes. "I'm waiting, Jake."

"Do I know anyone who would hurt Ryan? No, not really. But he must have been the one who painted over my walk board, which means he probably killed Debbie. Are you going to arrest him?"

"You're incorrigible, Jake. I asked you not to answer with another question," she said, smiling. "I'll bet you spent a lot of time in the corner when you were a kid."

"Sorry, Sarge."

She shook her head back and forth, causing her long hair to sway like in one of those shampoo commercials. "And you already know I don't like to be called that."

"Sorry, Sergeant, I forgot. But it's obvious he did it. Did you know she left him everything?" I could feel my ears burning.

Cruz shocked me by reaching over to touch my arm. "Calm down, Jake. You look like you're going to have a heart attack."

Her touch had its intended effect. I took a deep breath and let it out. "Okay, but you really need to bring him in for questioning."

She squeezed my arm before withdrawing her hand. "Unfortunately, that is out of the question. Unless you can speak to the dead, that is. He's at the morgue."

***

I called Bonnie from my cell phone the minute Cruz left the restaurant. "That's what she said, Bon. They found Ryan in the minivan at the Genesee rest area. Cruz said he must have been there at least twenty-four hours."

"More coffee, sweetheart?" It was the second time in less than ten minutes the waitress had asked. I couldn't get her attention when Sergeant Cruz had been here, and now she wouldn't leave me alone.

"Is Cruz still there?" Bonnie asked as I waved off the coffee.

"No, she left several minutes ago. It's my waitress. I'm at Denny's in Lakewood, if you want to join me."

"I'd love to, Jake, but Margot isn't doing well. I may have to stay with her a couple days. But tell me about Ryan. Do you think we'll have to return the retainer?"

"Under normal circumstances, I'd say it was the right thing to do."

"What does that mean, Jake?"

"These aren't normal circumstances. Not if we prove he pulled the trigger."

"Then it was suicide?" she asked.

"Not Ryan, Bon. Brendon. We need to prove that Brendon pulled the trigger. Ryan was shot between the eyes. I think they're ruling out suicide unless they find..." I paused when it looked like my waitress might drop her coffee pot. She had only managed to make it to the next table and evidently hadn't missed a single word of my conversation with Bonnie.

"Unless they find what, Jake?"

I turned my back to my nosey waitress before answering. "The minivan was set on fire after he was shot. I was going to say unless they find a pyromaniac that goes around looking for cars with dead people, it looks like whoever shot him tried to burn the evidence."

"Brendon Cole? You think he did it?"

"Who else had a motive?"

"So we can keep his money then?"

"I'm tempted, but we don't know for sure he did any of these murders, so I suppose we should return his retainer."

There was a pause on the other end, long enough for me to hear Margot in the background complaining about her tea. "It's a good thing I didn't spend any of it yet."

"Maybe not all of it, Bon. We do have our expenses."

"We do?"

"Of course. Take this breakfast for instance. You wouldn't believe how much that skinny little gal can eat."

"You bought her breakfast?"

"Best twelve dollars I ever spent. It's amazing how people open up over food. I went with the Value Slam myself. She started with something called a Santa Fe omelet and then ate my pancakes, but only after ordering strawberries to go with it. By the time she'd finished, there wasn't a scrap left for Fred, but that's okay--she kept talking about Ryan and Lisa the entire time."

Someone several tables down called my waitress and she had to miss out on the rest of my conversation. "Anyway, I'll give Brendon a call after I drive by Debbie's."

Once more I heard Margot in the background. "Thanks for calling, Jake. Margot needs me for something, but keep me up to date. I should be home in a couple days, so tell Fred he'll get all the table scraps he wants when I get back."

***

Debbie's house stood out for its lack of decorations. Halloween was just two days away and it was the only house on the block without ghosts hanging from its trees, or spider webs in the windows. I had a flash of melancholy when I saw the empty porch. I tried to picture Lisa in her cargo pants and baggy shirt, sitting on the top step. Fred must have had similar thoughts for he barked and wanted out when I pulled up to the curb.

"Easy, old fella, she's not here." He ran to the nearest tree the second I reached over and opened the passenger door.

I climbed the few stairs leading to the front door and rang the bell. The Westminster chimes told me the power was still on. I felt my pulse quicken at the thought of what I was about to do. Fred had joined me and was sitting calmly next to me. "What do you think, Freddie, should we get the rest of our tools before they become part of some probate?"

He turned his head to look at me. He didn't bark or whine. He just stared.

After several seconds of staring at each other I gave in, and knelt down to hold his head between my hands. "It's not like we're burglars. If I don't get those tools now I'll be out of business and you can forget about any more doggie treats."

This time he gave a short, soft bark, and licked my face. I hugged him, wiped my face with the sleeve of my shirt, and then got up to ring the bell again. I wanted to make sure no one was home before I went around back where Debbie had kept a key under a flower pot on the back porch. I looked up and down the street. It was deserted. Kids were in school and their parents at work. Still, it wasn't exactly the suburbs and not everyone on the street would be in school or at work.

The chimes hadn't struck three notes when I thought I saw movement through the beveled glass door. It was one of those ornate, solid mahogany doors with a half-glass, oval window. The window was designed to allow light into the foyer, while preventing anyone to see too clearly inside the house. What I couldn't see, Fred heard. He cocked his head in the direction of the door. It was all I needed to know that I hadn't imagined movement inside. My tools would have to wait for another day.

The decision to leave was reinforced when I saw a curtain move in the window of the house next door as I stepped onto the sidewalk. It was the house belonging to the woman Debbie had been fighting with before she died. I had never met the woman and decided it was time to introduce myself. But I did know that she hated dogs, cats, and most humans.

"Sorry, Freddie, but you better stay in the Jeep this time," I said to my sidekick and put him in the Jeep before heading to the neighbor's door.

Unlike the fancy door on Debbie's house, this one had no glass to let me peek through. Nor did it have a working doorbell, at least not one I could hear, so I knocked and waited. The results were the same as at Debbie's. What is it with these people? Are they all a bunch of recluses? Well, two can play that game. I'll sit in my Jeep and wait for them to come out.

I hadn't gone ten yards toward my Jeep when I heard the rumble of a big-block hemi coming from the alley behind Debbie's. I quickly jumped into my Jeep so I could race to the corner and see if it was the black Dodge Charger I'd seen yesterday.

"Not now, Freddie," I said when he wanted to kiss me again. He acted like I'd been gone a couple of days. The tone of my voice was enough to make him pout and jump in the back seat.

I felt bad, but didn't have time to apologize, and shoved the key in the Jeep's ignition. When the engine didn't start after a few seconds I pumped the gas pedal a couple times, only to smell the distinct odor of gasoline. I knew I'd given it too much gas, so I held the pedal to the floor and kept trying. "Damn it!" I yelled out loud. Fred jumped over another seat, putting as much distance between us as possible. I'm sure he would have gone out the back if the window had been open. This time I swore to myself when I heard the dreaded click of the starter. I'd drained the battery. The Charger, if that's what it was, would be long gone by the time the battery recovered enough to start my old Jeep.

I slammed my hand against the steering wheel and started to swear again. Then I saw Fred in the rear-view mirror, hunched in the corner.

"I'm sorry, Freddie. I'm not mad at you." I used the calmest voice I could muster.

His tail started thumping against the rear door.

I reached into the glove box where I kept a supply of doggie treats. "Come on up here you big oaf."

The treats seemed to work, Fred was by my side in record time, gulped down the first treat, and then begged me for more. I reached over and rubbed his head while giving him the last of the treats. "Does that mean you've forgiven me?" I asked. I didn't flinch when he answered by licking my face.

***

"What's his name, mister?" School must have let out its little gremlins. Several ghosts and goblins, as well a couple witches, had stopped to pet Fred as I sat on Debbie's front steps, waiting for Bonnie. I had called her after my battery refused to do its imitation of a zombie despite the fact that Halloween was only two days away. Actually, I had called her after AAA refused to come out because I'd used up my quota of service calls a few months back and failed to renew my contract.

"His name is Fred. Say hello, Fred."

There were six kids, along with an older teenager. The little girl who'd asked the question couldn't have been more than ten. Fred barked and held out his paw. This made all the kids giggle, except for one. A dark-skinned boy dressed in dirty jeans and a torn shirt looked like he was about to cry. He had been hiding behind the teenager who looked like she might be his sister.

She pushed him forward, toward Fred. "It's okay, Tanner. He won't bite you."

Tanner lowered his head and refused to look at Freddie.

"He's still upset about the witch next door, mister," said the teenager.

"The witch?" I asked.

One of the kids, dressed as the scarecrow from Oz, answered for her. "Crazy Mary." The kid's eyes were the size of a half dollars. "She poisoned Tanner's dog last month."

The teen added her two cents before her friend could elaborate. "Momma says it was antifreeze."

"It's her!" one of the kids yelled. Then they all screamed and ran down the street. I looked up in time to see the curtain close.

I had to hold Fred by his collar to stop him from running after the kids. He must have thought they wanted to play. "No, Freddie. It's not a game. Someone in that house spooked them. Maybe it's time we tried knocking on the door again."

We didn't get five feet when Bonnie's Cherokee pulled up to the curb.

"Just in time, Bon," I said, leaning into her open passenger window. "You can be my backup in case there are any fireworks."

"What?" She gave me the look I'd seen on the kid who'd told me the neighbor was known as Crazy Mary.

"Debbie's neighbor is playing hide and seek with us. We were just on our way over there. Rumor has it she isn't playing with a full deck, so get ready to call the cops if she shoots us."

"Jake! Are you crazy? If you don't care about yourself, at least think of Fred," she said, pointing at Fred. He had already worked himself between me and Bonnie. He had his big head in her window and his paws resting on the opening.

I looked at my pathetic dog, begging for Bonnie's attention, and then I looked over at the neighbor's house. "Yeah, you're right. I doubt if she'd answer anyway."

***

"By the way, how's Margot doing?" We were back at the same Denny's where I'd had breakfast earlier. Bonnie wasn't near as good looking as Sergeant Cruz, but she was a lot friendlier. I wouldn't trade her for a dozen Cruzes.

Bonnie put down her grilled cheese sandwich and looked at me. She looked worried, but tried to hide it. "As mean as ever. Thank you for rescuing me."

"That bad, huh?"

"Please tell me I'm not like her, Jake."

"As different as Evanora and Theodora."

"Who?"

"Two of the witches in Oz."

"Wasn't one of them called Glinda?"

"Glinda was a good witch. Evanora and Theodora were evil witches, and also sisters."

Bonnie pretended to pout. "So now I'm a witch, am I? See if I come to help you again."

"But a good witch, Bonnie, and just as beautiful as Glinda."

"Flattery will get you everywhere, mister. But to answer your question, there's nothing wrong with her that Jack can't fix."

"Jack?" I asked then hit myself on the side of my head with an open palm. "Oh, right. Mr. Daniels."

Bonnie's eyes lit up, and her smile was back. "If Margot would only lighten up and have a drink once in a while, she wouldn't be such a grouch." She started to take another bite of her sandwich, but had second thoughts. "And it wouldn't hurt you either, you know. You were a lot more fun when you were drinking."

"Let's not go there, Bon. You know I promised Julie."

She put down her sandwich down, and stared at her plate. "You really miss her, don't you?"

I had to change the subject before she started crying. Bonnie had loved Julie like a daughter and was nearly as upset as I had been when she died. "Well, I'm glad it's nothing serious, because we have work to do, if you're still part of my team."

She looked up with a blank look on her eyes and face. "Oh, you mean Margot," she said, playing with her fries. "No, nothing serious. I think she has a case of loneliness. And of course, I'm still part of the team. Do you have a new lead?"

"Do I ever. You won't believe what I heard from the peanut gallery today."

Chapter Fourteen

"Those two are up to something, Bon." I had told Bonnie about the Charger and the neighbor who wouldn't open her door while Bonnie finished her lunch. It took a while, not because it was such a long story, but because the same eavesdropping waitress I had earlier wouldn't let our coffee get cold.

"What makes you think they're in it together? We know Brendon had a motive to kill Debbie. He must have hated her when she won her lawsuit, and he lost his license," she said after wiping the last bit of sticky cheese from her lips. "But what's the neighbor's motive, Jake?'

"It's just a guess based on what the kids said about her. I know she and Debbie didn't get along. And for the record, he hasn't lost his license, it's only been suspended. But it's enough to put him out of business for the time being, so maybe Brendon paid her to kill Debbie so she couldn't testify against him."

"Hmm. I suppose that's possible, but my money's on him. What do you suppose he was looking for?"

"That, my dear lady, is what we will find out tomorrow."

Bonnie raised her eyebrows and tilted her head back a few inches. I waited for our waitress to move on before continuing. "Your nephew, Jonathan. I heard he quit the roofing business and now owns a carpet cleaning business."

She started to grin. "Yes, you heard right, and I have a good idea what you're thinking."

"You know me too well, Bon. So do you think he'll let me borrow a cleaning van?"

She was nearly jumping out of her seat with excitement. "I'll get Margot to tell him to let us use it. He can't turn down his own mother, especially when she pays the bills."

"Us? Don't you have to get back to helping Margot?"

"She'll survive a few hours without me."

I picked up our check and stood up. "Okay. See if you can get the van for tomorrow. We've got some serious cleaning to do."

"Let me get that, Jake," she said, reaching for the check.

I quickly put the check in my right hand, out of her reach. "No way, Bon. This one's on me. Brendon's check cleared and I sold a bunch of eBooks yesterday. It's my treat."

***

Bonnie went back to Margot's after leaving the restaurant, but not before stopping to see Fred and feed him the rest of her grilled cheese sandwich. He'd been sleeping in the back of my Wagoneer in a doggie bed Julie had bought him, but woke up before he could smell his treat. Our plan was for me to come back into town around noon tomorrow to pick up the cleaning van and the three of us would go back to Debbie's from there. I figured nobody would be suspicious of a cleaning crew. Even the nosey neighbor should think we had been called in to get the house ready to sell. I had no idea what we'd be looking for once inside. For all I knew Brendon had already found it, but at the very least, I'd be able to retrieve my tools.

I was halfway home when my cell phone rang. Caller ID said Cole Realty. Evidently Brendon hadn't bothered to change it even though he couldn't legally do business in Colorado.

"Hello?" was all I said. I thought I'd let him go first. Maybe he'd never heard the old adage about giving the guilty enough rope to hang themselves, so I decided to let him do just that and see how he was going to explain being at Debbie's.

"Jake?"

"Yes."

"It's me, Brendon Cole. I just called to see how the investigation is going."

"I was hoping you'd tell me."

"What's that mean, Jake?"

"What you were doing at Debbie's today?"

He didn't answer. I started to check the signal on my phone when he came back. "How'd you know it was me, Jake?"

"Good burglars don't drive cars that can be heard a block away and stick out like a possum in a chicken coop. So what were you doing there?"

"Oh. I think we need to talk."

"We *are* talking."

"I mean face to face. How's tomorrow morning? I'd come to your place, but last time it knocked my muffler loose. Do you mind coming into town?"

"Okay. Where and when?"

"How about my office at ten? The address is on the card I gave you."

"Ten works for me. I'll see you then." I found myself talking to nobody. Brendon had already disconnected.

I began to have second thoughts about meeting Brendon. There were already enough rude people in my life, and I didn't feel like dealing with another. But then I noticed I had no bars on my phone, and realized I was in a dead zone. The Genesee exit was up ahead, so I decided to pull off the freeway and try calling Bonnie from there.

We no sooner pulled into a small parking lot when I realized this must have been where Ryan was murdered. That brilliant deduction was confirmed by scorched asphalt in one of the parking spaces and a piece of yellow police tape wrapped around a nearby tree. All the spaces were taken now, except for the scorched one. It was next to a small picnic table and bench. At first I thought it was odd to see all the parked cars and not another soul, until I noticed the area was also a bus stop.

Fred jumped over my lap and headed for the nearest tree the second I opened my door. "Why didn't you say you had to go earlier, Freddie?" I said as I walked over to him. He was too busy barking to answer me. Then I saw it wasn't a call of nature that had him so upset. A small herd of bison were staring him down from the other side of the parking lot.

"I think you've met your match with those guys, Fred." I reached down to grab his collar in case he decided to do more than bark. He wasn't having any part of it and pulled away before I got a firm grip, and ran back toward the Jeep. I could tell he wanted to play. He'd been cooped up in the Jeep far too long, and when I got close to him again he ran over to the picnic table, daring me to give chase. Then suddenly, as though someone had flipped a switch, he stopped running and began sniffing the air. I watched as he slowly made his way to a trash can next to the picnic table. He turned to look at me and barked.

"Did someone put something good in there, Freddie," I asked when I caught up with him.

He barked again and pointed his nose toward the trash can.

I knew he wouldn't stop until I checked it out, so after making sure we were still alone, I opened the lid, looked inside, then turned back to Fred in awe. He was sitting on his haunches, smiling. "You really amaze me sometimes," I said, kneeling down to his level so I could rub the hair on his head.

**

Maybe I'd given Fred too much credit. I'd assumed he knew the pile of yellow wrappers was from the same butterscotch candy Brendon had when he visited us at our cabin, but it was more likely Fred had smelled the half-eaten Big Mac on top of the wrappers. The burger was infested with maggots, which told me it had been there at least a couple of days – about the time Ryan was killed. I put a few of the candy wrappers in my pocket before calling Bonnie.

Chapter Fifteen

Bonnie agreed to meet me at Brendon's office in Lakewood when I called and told her about our change of plans. She didn't seem to be too upset that we wouldn't be cleaning any carpets.

As usual, she was late and I was early, but not earlier than Brendon. His Charger was parked in a spot under one of the few trees in the parking lot. I pulled in next to it and waited for Bonnie. His card claimed he had an office on the main floor of a three-story office building. There were several identical buildings, collectively called Denver West-- not exactly the kind of place I'd expect to see a real estate office. I decided to let Fred out while we waited for Bonnie.

Putting Fred on a leash wasn't necessary. These were office buildings, not stores, and seeing as we were the only ones in the parking lot, I let him out of the Jeep. He went straight to Brendon's car. I almost called him back, afraid of what he'd do next, when he started to sniff at the wheels. When he didn't lift a leg, I let him be until he went over to the driver's door and barked.

I quickly went over to see what he'd found. "What is it, Freddie?" He stood up on his hind legs, put his paws on the door, and looked into the car. Almost immediately, an alarm went off.

"Uh-oh, now you've done it." I barely had time to say it before Fred ran back to our Jeep with his tail between his legs. I wasn't far behind. If I'd had a tail, I'm sure I'd look a lot like Fred.

My first thought after getting into the Jeep with Fred was to get away from the wailing alarm as fast as I could. Of course, that'd make matters worse, and I'd probably be pulled over before I managed to make it back to I-70. I also knew there'd be a good chance I'd flood the carburetor and drain the battery, so I decided to sit and wait for security to arrive. "Well, this is another fine mess you've gotten us into, Freddie," I said, looking at him lying in the passenger seat, his head between his paws.

He looked up at me with his big brown eyes like he didn't have a clue as to what I was saying.

I reached over to fluff up the hair on his head. "So what's in there that was so interesting?"

He responded by tilting his head to the side. He was telling me he wanted his ears scratched. I obliged and waited for someone to call security, or worse, the cops. My old, beat-up Wagoneer, sitting next to a sixty-thousand dollar vehicle, should have several people inside watching us, and dialing 911 to report an attempted car theft.

Luckily, I didn't have to wait around to answer questions while lying on the ground with my hands behind my back in cuffs. Bonnie showed up about the same time the alarm stopped. I was out of my Jeep and leading her into the building before she could say hello. Fred would have to explain why he'd set off the alarm without my help.

***

"You look like you've seen a ghost, Jake," she said once we were inside and I slowed down to catch my breath. I'd expected to see a guard behind a desk in the middle of the lobby with his gun drawn, but there wasn't one. There wasn't even an information desk.

"Fred set off the alarm on Brendon's car just before you got here. I expect the place will be crawling with cops before long."

Bonnie laughed. "You've been watching too many movies, Jake. Nobody pays any attention to those."

I took a quick look outside without reminding her I didn't have a TV. She was right of course. Everything was back to normal. Even Fred had laid down to take a nap. Or maybe he was hiding, but either way, he had nothing to worry about. No one seemed to hear car alarms anymore.

"How'd he manage to set off the alarm?" She was holding a small purse in front of her with both hands. Unlike me, she seemed to be in her element. I'd never seen her dressed in such expensive clothing before, and assumed the blue pants-suit and pearl necklace were borrowed from her sister.

"He put his big paws on the door frame so he could look inside. Brendon must have one of those pressure sensitive alarms. It went off before I could see what Fred thought was so interesting."

She reached out and took my arm. "Well, shall we go inside and see how Brendon's going to explain what he was doing in Debbie's house?"

Brendon Cole's office didn't look like any real estate office I'd ever seen. A lawyer would be more at home in it than any salesman. "Can I offer you a butterscotch?" he said, pointing to a jar of the yellow candies on his huge, mahogany desk after we'd sat down in a couple of red, leather seats. I felt a pang of envy when I thought about the kitchen table I used for writing.

He took one for himself before passing us the jar.

"Maybe for later," Bonnie said, taking several and putting them into her purse.

I passed, waving him off. "Before we get started, Brendon, I should tell you that Fred accidently set off your car alarm."

He laughed, simultaneously ripping open the wrapper on his butterscotch. "I really need to get that thing fixed, or at the least stop parking under that tree. The squirrels have set it off so many times that nobody pays any attention to it anymore. Someone could steal it out from under me and I'd never know."

I looked over at Bonnie in time to see a huge grin on her face before she covered her mouth with her hand. "Then I guess we can get down to business. You said you could explain why you were inside Debbie's house?"

Brendon let his eyes drop to a notepad on his desk. I had already tried to read it, but there was nothing but doodles on it. "I had hoped to find Debbie's sister there and the temptation to let myself in was too great."

"Lisa? She went back to Kansas City," I said.

He stopped doodling and looked up. "Or so they say. I've left her more messages than I can count."

"Why's that?" Bonnie asked, leaning forward.

He turned toward Bonnie, looking like a kid being questioned by his teacher. "I never had much luck with Debbie or Ryan, but now that she stands to inherit the estate, I was hoping we could come to some kind of settlement."

"But that still doesn't explain why you let yourself in." Bonnie held up both her index fingers in the universal sign for quotation marks as I said the word in.

I cut in before he could answer. "Whoa, hold up a minute. You know about Ryan being killed?"

"Of course, Jake. It's all over the news. Well, except for Fox. All they want to talk about is Trump's temper and Hillary's emails."

Bonnie laughed and started to say something before I cut her off. The last thing we needed now was a political discussion. "No, I don't have a TV. I mean, I didn't hear it on the news, but we did know about it."

Bonnie gave me her hurt look before turning to Brendon and adding her two cents worth. "So with Debbie and Ryan out of the way, you thought you could make a deal with Lisa by breaking into her house?"

Brendon lowered his eyes and unwrapped another butterscotch.

"She's got a point there, Brendon," I said, watching him play with his candy. "What were you really doing in there?"

He finally popped the candy into his mouth and looked me in the eyes. "Rumor has it those letters you found could prove Lisa's not the rightful heir."

Bonnie's eyes nearly popped out of her head. "How'd you hear about them?" she asked.

There was a slight hesitation before he answered. "Her boyfriend, Ryan, made some remark about how she wasn't really Debbie's sister."

"Her boyfriend?" Bonnie asked. "You mean Debbie's boyfriend, don't you?"

"He was Debbie's boyfriend. Evidently Lisa inherited him along with everything else. When I asked why he thought Lisa wasn't the heir, he said you had found some letters proving she was the illegitimate child of a boarder."

Bonnie started to say something, so I gave her a slight kick with my foot. I didn't want her telling Brendon that I had the letters. "And that would nullify her claim to the estate?" I asked. Bonnie gave me a dirty look, but luckily, Brendon had gone back to doodling and missed it.

"Maybe," he answered. He set his pen down and reached for another butterscotch. "You scared me off before I could get started. I didn't know it was you. I thought it might be the nosey neighbor, so I never had a chance to look for the letters."

It looked like he had more to say, so I waited. Bonnie sat back in her chair and wouldn't look at either of us. "So now I need you more than ever, Jake," he said, while unwrapping his candy. "I'd be willing to pay dearly if you can find that letter for me."

Bonnie stopped pouting at the mention of payment and spoke, but not before moving her legs out of the reach of my foot. "And how much is, dearly?"

Brendon was all smiles again. "What say another thousand?"

"Each?" she asked.

"Yes, each. And another grand apiece if you deliver."

***

Bonnie made a show of rubbing her leg while I put her coffee on the table. This time we'd gone to the Starbuck's inside Barnes and Nobel only a few blocks from Brendon's office. "Sorry about that, Bon. You gonna be okay?"

"I'll live. I may never walk again, but I'll live." Her smile said more than her words. "So why didn't you want Brendon to know you have the letters? I'm glad you stopped me, or he may not have given us another check, but what's the big secret?"

I gave her the biggest Andy Taylor grin I could manage. "Well, Barn, or should I call you Aunt Bee? I didn't have a chance to tell you before the meeting, but Fred found some evidence earlier that proves Brendon is a pathological liar and murderer. That jar of candy on his desk confirmed my suspicions."

"What?" Lucky for her the coffee had been too hot to hold, or she might have dropped it.

"Fred found several of those candy wrappers at the parking area where Ryan was murdered."

"No way, Jose. When were you there?"

"Yesterday, when I called you. I pulled off I-70 to get better reception and let Fred stretch his legs. They have a little picnic area there, with a table, and trash can by the bus stop. He smelled something delicious in the trash can. The wrappers were under a maggot infested burger. Those ugly bugs mean the wrappers were thrown away about the same time Ryan met his maker."

"And Brendon is addicted to butterscotch candy." Bonnie finished the sentence for me.

"Exactly."

"Then why on earth did you promise to help him? Shouldn't we be going to the police?"

"And have Cruz slap my hand again? We need more proof than the fact he likes butterscotch candy. That's why I played him along until I can give him enough rope to hang himself with."

She seemed to consider what I'd said. She looked like Rodin's Thinker, with her hand supporting her chin. Except I don't remember him holding a cup of Starbuck's coffee in his free hand. "And how do you plan on being a hangman?"

"Well, from what I see, he's already tied the noose."

"Enough with the metaphors, Jake. Can you tell me without sounding like a Freshman English student?"

I pretended to pout, but my smile gave me away. "The letters, Bon. Debbie never read them. So how was she able to tell Ryan about the illegitimate child?"

Bonnie's knuckles went white from holding her coffee cup too tight. "Then how could Brendon possibly know what's in the letters if we're the only ones who have read them?"

"We've been assuming they were left there by a border during the Second World War. That was our first mistake. What if Brendon put them there?"

Her cup finally collapsed from the pressure of her grip. Fortunately, it was empty. She ignored the cup and stared at me.

"He certainly had access when he was her realtor. You know what I think?"

"No, damn it! Tell me before I have to change my Depends."

"I doubt if Mary Johnson even exists. I think Brendon wrote them, or had someone write them for him, to make it look like Debbie's grandfather had fathered Mary's child."

"Why would he do that?"

"Probate, Bon. My research revealed that Debbie's mother inherited the house because there was no will and she was the only child. But if it turns out the grandfather had another kid, wouldn't he or she be entitled to an equal share?"

"I suppose, but I still don't see what that has to do with the price of tea in China?"

"You're showing your age, Bon. I haven't heard that since I was a kid. It was one of my dad's favorite expressions."

Bonnie wrinkled her lip and came close to sticking out her tongue out at me.

"The tea I'm speaking of is the lawsuit. I doubt if it's valid if Debbie doesn't own the house."

"That's a lot of ifs, Jake. You remind me of my Greg. He used to fish with four or five poles, each pole with a different bait or lure. He wanted to be sure he'd catch whatever was biting that day."

I had to laugh, for my theories were akin to fishing. "And you say I talk in metaphors. But if Brendon didn't plant the letters, tell me how he knew what was in them? Remember Debbie told me to throw them in the trash. She never bothered to look at them."

Her eyebrows went up and she sat straighter in her chair. "That's right, mister genius. I didn't catch that slip-up." Then her face went blank. "But that doesn't make sense either. Why would he plant letters to get her lawsuit dismissed when he must have known she'd be the one to find them? All she'd have to do is burn them and keep quiet."

"Precisely why he was in the house. He wasn't looking for letters, he was planting new ones, and now he thinks I'm dumb enough to go back inside the house and discover more letters that I missed the first time."

"So are you?"

"You just called me a genius and now you're asking if I'm dumb?"

"No, silly. Are you going to go back in and get the letters?"

"Of course. Do you think we can still get Jonathan's cleaning van?"

"I'll call Margot and see." Bonnie giggled and began searching her purse. I knew it would take several minutes before she found her phone, so I slid mine across the table.

"Use mine, Bon. It'll be quicker."

She frowned and went back to digging through her huge purse. "I don't know her number."

I took her answer to mean she had Margot's number programmed into her phone and let it go.

"Here it is," she said, grinning. It was an ancient flip phone that made me wonder if it was connected to Margot with a string. I took the opportunity to refill our coffee while Bonnie talked to her sister, for I knew they would have to discuss everything but borrowing the van first.

***

Bonnie wasn't a happy camper when I returned with our coffee. "What's the long face for, Bon," I asked, setting her coffee down after adjusting the anti-burn wrapper they put on the cups.

"You'll have to go without me or the van, Jake. Jonathan won't let us use it and Margot needs me. She's going in for a heart cath tomorrow."

Chapter Sixteen

"I need you to be my lookout, Freddie," I said after I parked in the alley behind Debbie's house and her neighbors'. She had a detached, single-car garage in the back, facing the alley. There had been a fence to keep people from the alley out of her yard, but I had removed that when the dumpster was brought in and was fired before I had a chance to put it back. I was able to get close to the back porch, and hence the flower pot where Debbie hid a key to the house, without being seen by the neighbors.

Fred had other ideas. He had been left in the Jeep too long when I was at the coffee shop, and now he wanted out. The last thing I needed was for him to bark and alert the neighbor, so I let him out of the Jeep. "Can you be quiet and promise to behave?"

He answered with a loud bark. I might as well have asked him to run over and knock on Crazy Mary's door.

"Shh, Freddie," I said and bent down to his level so we could talk. "Do you want her calling the cops on us?"

He barked again, only this time I looked up to see why. "Lisa? You're back?"

"How could I stay away from my two favorite guys?" she said from the back porch. She had been sitting on the top step, much like she had the day I'd first met her. Only this time it was the rear of the house, and she wasn't wearing her khakis with the big pockets. She had on loose shorts and a Royal's sweatshirt.

Fred broke loose from my grip and ran toward her wagging his tail.

"I missed you, too, Freddie," she said, leaning down to ruffle his hair.

"You weren't thinking of breaking into my house, where you, Jake?" Her smile assured me she hadn't called the cops...yet.

"I seem to have lost my Sawzall. I must have left it here. I tried calling you a hundred times. When did you get back?"

She moved over to make room for Fred. The big ham loved every minute of the massage she was giving his neck. "This morning," she answered, lowering her eyes. Her smile drifted away with her gaze. "I wanted to call you back, Jake, but I couldn't."

I went over to the stairs and sat crossways on the bottom step. "Hey, it's not like we're married. I just wanted to know what happened to you."

She took a deep breath and sighed. "I lied about having to get back to work. The truth is, Jake, I *am* married."

Fred sensed the change in her mood and put a paw on her lap.

It brought her smile back, but only for a moment. "We haven't been getting along for some time. I thought the trip out here would give me a chance to clear my head. I didn't expect to meet someone like you."

Fred let out a short bark that made her laugh again. "And you, too, Freddie."

She pretended to whisper in his ear, just loud enough so I could hear. "Don't tell your master, but I missed *you* the most."

I hadn't thought about another woman since Julie died and now that I found one I really liked, I find she's married. I had to cut this off before it went any further. "Well, I'm glad you're okay. I was afraid whoever shot Ryan might have done the same to you, too."

She stopped petting Fred and looked up. "Someone killed Ryan?"

"In your minivan. It's why I kept calling you."

"Oh, my God. I've been so mad at him because I had to rent a car to get here from the airport when he wouldn't answer my calls. How horrible."

I inadvertently glanced over at the garage, wondering where she'd parked the rental. "Then you didn't know?"

"No. This is the first I've heard of it," she answered, getting up.

I rose as well, but Fred didn't. He looked up at Lisa, reminding me of one of Dickens' street urchins begging for a handout. "So is it okay if I look for my saw?"

"Sure," she answered. I thought she was going to lead the way into the house, but she picked up a tennis ball that had been stuck under the porch rail and threw it. Fred went after it before it cleared the porch. "You know the house better than I do, Jake. I'll stay here with Fred while you get your stuff."

***

The back door led into a room that might have been a washroom at one time. There was a huge, cement sink that must have served as a place for servants to wash clothes. I doubt if Debbie had ever used it, for there was a matching front-loading washer and dryer next to the sink. Next to the dryer was a free-standing cupboard. I'd seen one like it on an antique shopping trip with Julie. She had called it a Hoosier cabinet. I wasted no time searching it for the letter I was sure Brendon had left for me to find.

"That's a funny place to put a saw." I'd been so intent in my search, I didn't hear Lisa and Fred come inside. I closed the cabinet drawer and turned around. She was standing with her hands on her hips and a frown on her face. She didn't look happy.

Fred sensed the change as well and came over to attach himself to my thigh. "Damn, you scared me, Lisa. I didn't hear you come in."

Her eyes narrowed. I had to think fast before she literally blew up. "Out of sight, out of mind," I said, moving away from the cabinet. "I put my more valuable tools in there where another worker couldn't see them."

Her hands went from her hips to under her biceps as she crossed her arms. "Well, please don't go through any more antiques unless you ask. That's been sold to a dealer in Loveland and he wouldn't be too happy if you broke it on him."

"You sold it?"

"Yes, and most of the other antiques, as well. I plan on having a garage sale for the rest of it."

"But you said you just got here. How did you manage to find buyers so soon?"

She uncrossed her arms, dropping her hands to her side. "I took pictures before going back to Missouri and put them on Craigslist, not that it's any of your business."

I began to wonder if Lisa was bipolar. Ten minutes ago it looked like she wanted me to hop into bed with her and now she acted like I'd run over her cat. "Sorry, I didn't mean to get you upset. I'll just run upstairs. Maybe I left the saw in the bedroom I was working on. I promise I won't look inside any more cabinets."

I didn't wait for her answer and headed toward the servant's stairs. It was a feature the finer homes had when the upper-middle-class could afford servants. They didn't want the hired help to be seen unless they were called. Fred didn't need to be told to follow--he was still attached to my leg.

"Now will you try to earn your keep and guard the stairs for me?" I whispered to Fred once we'd made it to the third level. Lisa had stayed behind. I'd seen her walk over to her precious Hoosier cabinet when we had reached the second level. It was a U-shaped staircase that required a change in direction at each level, giving me a clear view of her as she checked out the cabinet.

Fred didn't argue with me this time, so I went down the hall toward the bedroom where I'd found the first letters. I turned around before entering the bedroom to see Fred looking sadder than a seal locked up in a pen, but he hadn't moved an inch.

"Where would I hide something I wanted to be found?" I said to myself.

I was about to answer myself when I saw it. Another letter, exactly where the armoire had been, stuffed behind some exposed lath with just enough envelope exposed so it could be found by even a failing Braille student. I quickly extracted the letter from the wall, put it in my waistband, and pulled my undershirt and sweatshirt over it. Fred barked just as I finished.

"Did you find it?" Her tone had suggested she was no longer upset with me.

I had found what I'd come for, so it was time to gather my flock and go. "No. I'm sorry I bothered you, Lisa. Maybe it's buried in my shed somewhere. I'm not exactly the best-organized handyman. Fred and I'll get going before we do break something valuable."

Lisa closed the distance between us and reached out for my hand. She looked up at me without saying a word and wrapped her arms around my neck.

The kiss only lasted a second and then she was gone. I stood there, immobilized and confused. I could feel hormones swimming through my body that I thought had died. Then I looked over at Fred who had seen it all. He just sat there, looking at me with a wicked grin. "What are you looking at, you grungy mutt?" I swear his grin grew wider.

I soon forgot Fred and let my thoughts drift back to Lisa. Did she want me to follow her? Part of me wanted to, but I couldn't. I'd let my hormones make the mistake of getting involved with a married woman once before and still felt guilty about it, even though I knew that marriage had been long over. Lisa solved the dilemma for me when I heard the back door slam shut. I looked out the window in time to see her going over to Crazy Mary's.

Chapter Seventeen

"Dear Michael, I don't know how to say this so I'll come straight to the point. I miscarried last night. I'm sure you already knew the baby wasn't yours, so at least now you won't have to raise a child you didn't father. Please forgive me. Your loving wife, Mary." I read Bonnie the letter over the phone. I had tried giving her a brief synopsis of it on my way up I-70, but she insisted I pull over and read it in its entirety.

"Is that all?"

"That's it," I said after putting the letter in my glove box, and pulling back into traffic. Almost immediately the driver of a Cadillac Escalade let me know he wasn't happy by leaning on his horn a little too long.

"That doesn't make sense, Jake. The last letter you found said the baby had already been born," Bonnie said over the noise of the Cadillac.

"You catch on quick, Bon."

Silence. I could only imagine the nasty looks she must be giving me. "Just because I didn't choose to work for NASA after college doesn't mean I'm stupid. We can't all be rocket scientists."

"Sorry, Bon. I didn't mean it that way. And I was a programmer, not a rocket scientist."

"You're forgiven, sonny. But tell me why Brendon would forge such a stupid letter. It does nothing to invalidate Debbie's lawsuit, and I don't need to be a lawyer to see that."

"It kind of blows my theory about him exposing the illegitimate child, doesn't it?"

"Then Brendon didn't plant the letter?"

"Not unless he's some kind of masochist, Bon. It only confirms Lisa's right to the estate. I..." The Cadillac cut in front of me, nearly clipping the front of my Jeep. "Whoa, that was close," I said. Then the driver did the unthinkable and slammed on his brakes.

In less time than it takes the atomic clock to measure a nanosecond, I hit my brakes to avoid the jerk in front of me. Unfortunately, the guy behind me didn't have the same reflexes, and I felt my head snap forward, and then slam back into the headrest. Fred didn't have the restraint of a seatbelt so he didn't get his head whipped like a tether ball. He'd been sleeping on the rear seat and got slammed into the back of my seat instead. I pulled back onto the shoulder to get off the freeway, and the guy who hit me did the same.

***

"Are you okay, man?" He looked to be about half my age, maybe in his mid-twenties, with a shaved head and untrimmed, blond beard with tobacco stains. He was standing outside my Jeep's window looking whiter than an anemic vampire. I had been too busy checking Fred for broken bones to see him approach.

When Fred didn't complain about his examination, I turned to the man at my window, rubbed the back of my neck, and got out of my Jeep. "We'll live. How about you? Is there anyone else in your car?"

"Just me, man, and I'm good. Can't say the same for my airbag or the rest of the car. Who was that idiot?"

"No idea," I said, walking to the rear of my Jeep. "He must have been upset that I didn't leave him enough room when I pulled out into traffic. I thought I had plenty of time to get up to speed, but that was before I realized he must have been doing over eighty."

My Jeep was going to need a new tailgate and bumper, but his old Subaru wasn't going anywhere but the junk yard. He turned his head to spit before continuing. "Looks like I got the worst of it, bud. I hope you got good insurance."

"Just liability, but I doubt if I'll need it. I do believe when the cops get here they will find you at fault."

All of a sudden his attitude changed. His eyes looked like they might pop out of their sockets and he laughed. It wasn't the kind of laugh one makes after hearing a joke, but rather one with an edge. A mean edge. "What the hell you talking about, man? You're the one who's at fault, not me."

"Hey, don't have a cow. Why don't we exchange insurance information and wait for the Highway Patrol to show up? I'm sure if he thinks I'm at fault I'll be the one who gets the ticket, not you."

"Ticket?" he asked, looking away from me, toward the traffic coming up the hill. "Uh, hey, no need to get The

Man involved. Why don't you just give me your insurance info and let them handle it."

"It's in my glove box. I'll get it and a notepad so I can write yours down, too. But we'll still need to wait for the trooper."

His anger seemed to have subsided and now he couldn't look me in the eyes. "Uh, yeah. I'll go get mine. It's in the car"

Fred was all smiles when I went to his door. He must have thought I was going to let him out. "Not now, Freddie. I just need something out of the glove box. Do you mind moving over?" I said, rubbing his head.

He didn't move out of the way, and before I could push him over I heard the Subaru start up and tear out into traffic. "What the..." I said, slamming Fred's door and running around to the driver's side. "We need to get his license number, Freddie."

I was in the driver's seat, cranking the engine quicker than Fred could tree a squirrel. I was also just as successful as he was with his squirrels. Once again, the old Jeep wouldn't start. This time I couldn't blame it on anyone but myself. The low gas warning light had been on since I'd left town, and now the gas-gauge needle didn't move a millimeter.

Chapter Eighteen

Bonnie shook the bottle of ibuprofen like a baby's rattle. "I still say you should see a doctor, Jake. You could have whiplash for all you know." We were sitting on my deck having our morning coffee, and she'd just made me take another pill. Margot's heart cath had been postponed, so Bonnie had decided Fred and I needed nursing more than Margot. She'd come back when I called her to tell her about the hit and run.

She looked down at Fred who was lying between us. "And you're sure he's okay?"

"We're okay, Bon, honest. It wasn't that bad."

"I saw your Jeep, sonny, don't tell me it wasn't that bad. I'm surprised either of you can still walk."

"We could run a marathon if we had to. The vet said X-rays didn't show anything broken, but she said to keep an eye on him just the same. I would have asked her to x-ray my neck, too, if I'd known you were going to make such an issue of it."

She put the pills in her purse and sat back in her chair. "You amaze me, Jake."

"Why's that, Bon?"

"You won't go to the ER to be checked out, but you made sure Fred did. Where did you even find a vet open yesterday?"

"We went to that animal clinic on Ward Rd. It cost me everything Brendon paid me, but it's worth it knowing he's not hurt."

The grooves in her forehead went from wrinkles to miniature Grand Canyons. "I'd nearly forgotten about him. Are you going to give him that letter?"

"No. Not yet."

Bonnie leaned closer, licking her lips. She was either anxiously waiting for the punch line, or thinking about becoming a cannibal.

"It's not real, Bon."

She picked up the letter and envelope from the deck table. "It sure looks real. I haven't seen envelopes this thin since I was a little girl. My mama told me that was to cut down on the weight when airmail was so expensive in the forties. And what about this stamp and postmark? How could anyone forge those?"

I pointed to the letter she had extracted from the envelope. "Oh, the envelope's real all right. Someone took the original letter and replaced it with that forgery."

Bonnie adjusted her reading glasses and took a closer look. She put it up to her nose and sniffed it. "I don't think so, smarty. You'd be able to smell the ink; they used fountain pens back then."

"Precisely, Bon. That's the mistake the forger made. You can't smell the ink because he used a ballpoint pen. I did some research last night and found they didn't come into common use until the fifties. The ballpoint was invented in 1935 but was too expensive and not really perfected until the early fifties."

Bonnie removed her glasses and let them drop to her chest where they swung like a pendulum. "There you go, again. Why is it always a he? Who has the most to gain by this letter?"

I paused for a second before answering. She was right, but all I could think about was the kiss Lisa had given me. "Lisa?"

Bonnie gave me her Cheshire cat grin, and didn't say a word.

"Okay, she definitely has a motive, means, and opportunity, but I really thought she was smarter than that. I'm sure it won't take a forensics lab five minutes to verify the ink is fresh. She probably found some old stationary and used an envelope from another letter, but surely she must have realized the ink would expose the letter as a fraud."

"I wonder what the original letter said." From her tone and posture, I could tell Bonnie wasn't really asking, but simply thinking out loud. Her head had been propped up by her right hand with the elbow resting on the edge of my table. Then her elbow slipped and her head bobbed like one of those bobble-head dolls on a dashboard.

"Are you okay, Bon?"

"That's it, Jake!"

It was my turn to stare.

"She found the letter Brendon planted and replaced it with this forgery. We've got to find the original."

"Whoa. Hold on there, Pilgrim. If Brendon planted a letter, wouldn't it be a forgery, too?"

"What are you saying, Jake?"

"Maybe he didn't plant a letter. It's possible he was telling me the truth about being in the house, looking for the letter that would disinherit both Debbie and Lisa. You know, the one I found where Mary Johnson mentions having a baby that couldn't possibly be her husband's because he had been overseas for thirteen months. That should be all the proof he needs to get a new trial. It means the sisters aren't the only ones who have a claim to the estate."

Bonnie's eyes grew to the size of small plates. "Which means he knew about the letters. And how would he know that… unless Ryan told him just before Brendon did him in."

Her excitement made me smile. She reminded me so much of my sister when we played hide and seek so many years ago. Megan, my sister, had outgrown that exuberance, but Bonnie still had it. "Except Ryan couldn't have known about the letters, Bon. How could he? He would have had to get that information from Debbie, and she never read them. Remember, she told me to throw them in the trash after I'd found them?"

"Oh, Jake. You're such a fool when it comes to women. Did you ever think that maybe Debbie set you up? What if she had found the letter before you, and told you to throw it away knowing you'd read it and never suspect she knew?"

"I'll have to agree on one of your points, Bon. I'll never understand what makes women tick, but if Debbie knew what was in the letters, she'd have burned them before anyone else could read them."

Bonnie narrowed her eyes and jutted her chin forward. I could tell she was not ready to give up her argument, any more than a gator wrestler would stick his hand down the throat of a fifteen-foot alligator. "Then it was Ryan."

I could feel my brow wrinkle. "Ryan? Oh, we're back to Ryan killing Debbie? I thought we were talking about the letters."

"Of course, silly. I know you're not sixteen anymore, but try to keep up with me. Ryan must have killed Debbie, then killed himself when his conscience got the better of him."

"Only two thing wrong with that theory, Bon."

"Oh?"

"Well, number one is the gun. If Ryan killed himself, wouldn't they have found the gun in the minivan? But more importantly, how did he manage to burn the van *after* shooting himself?"

"He started the fire before pulling the trigger and then threw the gun out of the car, and someone came along and took it. Not only are they hard to come by, but they're damn expensive as well." Bonnie turned away abruptly and looked down at Fred. "Would you tell your Doubting Thomas master that some of us don't need a mountain of scientific evidence to believe in something."

Up until that point, Fred didn't seem to care what we were saying. But he knew when Bonnie was upset, so he looked over at her and barked.

I reached down to pet him while considering what Bonnie had said. It was possible Ryan killed Debbie, but I wasn't buying his suicide, or Debbie planting the letter for me to find. That didn't make any sense. She had nothing to gain and everything to lose if anyone found out about the letter that would put her inheritance in jeopardy, which brought me back to my original suspect, Brendon. "Let's start over, Bon. All these letters are connected somehow, and we need to go about it logically if we want to figure this out."

She fumbled around in her purse and brought out a pack of cigarettes. "Do you mind, Jake? It helps me think."

I nodded okay. "First, there was the letter sent after Michael Johnson was killed in action. Then the letter Mary wrote, but never mailed, about the illegitimate child. And now this forgery saying that child died before being born, which we know is a lie, because it contradicts Mary's letter."

Bonnie inhaled deeply and held it a few seconds before exhaling. "I really needed that, Jake. Go on."

"Okay. Let's get back to motive. Who has the most to gain by Debbie's death?"

Bonnie held her cigarette in mid-air, ready to take another drag. "Before or after Ryan was killed? At first I'd say him, but with him out of the way, it's got to be Lisa."

The vision of Lisa kissing me with her arms wrapped around my neck wouldn't go away. "I'll grant you Lisa has a good motive, but she was in Missouri when Debbie was killed."

"Then it was Ryan, which means I was right when I said he killed himself."

"Are we forgetting Brendon?"

"I thought you said you didn't suspect him any longer, Jake."

"I don't know what to think, Bon. He'd be nuts to plant a letter that eliminates a third heir, so maybe he was looking for Mary's letter, but then how did he know about it?"

Bonnie pushed back her chair and looked down at Fred. "What do you think, Freddie? Is Brendon a bad guy or not?"

Fred looked up at her and barked.

"I think that's a yes, Jake."

"Thanks a lot, Freddie," I said, giving him my disappointed stare.

He put his head back down between his paws.

I had to reach down and pat him on his head. "Sorry, boy, I'm not mad at you. I was only joking."

His tail started wagging and he raised his head, smiling. It made me wonder who the joker really was. I didn't have long to wonder before my phone started ringing. "It's Sergeant Cruz, Bon," I said after looking at the caller ID.

Chapter Nineteen

Sergeant Cruz was already at Debbie's house when Bonnie, Fred, and I drove up. I hadn't fixed the tail lights on my Jeep yet, so we all went in Bonnie's Cherokee.

"I didn't expect you to bring your entourage," she said when she met us at the front door. Her lips had been pressed tightly together before speaking, and she looked annoyed. Then she looked down at Fred who was sitting next to me with his head down. "I'm sorry, big fella. I'm always happy to see you."

Fred held out his paw for a handshake, causing the sergeant to smile. She bent down and gently took his paw before turning back to me. "Well, I'm glad you could meet me on such short notice. Do you have the letter?"

"Yes," I said, handing it to her. "Do you mind if I ask how you knew about it?"

She looked over the letter very carefully then stuck it in a breast pocket of her blazer. "I'll tell you that, Jake, if you'd be kind enough to tell me where you found the letters."

"In the bedroom I was remodeling."

"We know that, Jake. Do you mind showing us?" She didn't wait for me to answer and went back into the house, leaving the door open for us.

She was already halfway up the main staircase when we let ourselves into the foyer. I looked over at Bonnie and shrugged before heading toward the stairs. Fred and I caught up with the sergeant, who was standing outside the bedroom where Debbie had died, before Bonnie had even made it to the first landing. "After you, Jake," she said, waving her hand in the universal motion for me to go on in.

I was surprised to see her partner. I'd assumed she had meant Lisa when she'd said 'us' earlier. He was looking at the holes in the wall where I had started removing the lath and plaster before Debbie had fired me. He stopped his examination the moment we walked in. "Mr. Martin," he said, turning to greet us. "Is this where you found the letters?"

I looked over at Sergeant Cruz for some kind of confirmation just as she opened her blazer to show Hopkins the letter I'd given her.

She must have noticed my surprise. "I'm sorry, Jake. You remember my partner, Sergeant Hopkins?"

"Yes. Good to see you again, Sergeant."

"Yeah, right," he answered, rolling his eyes. "So where are the other letters now?"

Bonnie came into the room before I could answer. "The owner told him to throw them in the dumpster, so he did."

Everyone turned to look at Bonnie. Hopkins spoke first. "Who are you?"

"She's Mr. Martin's neighbor, Bill. It's okay. They're sort of a team."

Hopkins relaxed a bit, but now had his arms crossed. "And the dog? Did you ask them to bring the dog, too?"

"Without Fred you'd never know about the message." I'd almost expected to see Bonnie pout after she spoke. She sounded closer to six than she did seventy.

Hopkins' eyes grew large. "Fred?" Then he looked down at Fred and his eyes went back to normal. "Oh. That's a strange name for a dog."

"He had a sister named Ginger, Sherlock," Bonnie said. "What's so strange about that?"

Sergeant Cruz held up her hands in the universal sign of time-out. "I'm sure Sergeant Hopkins meant no harm, Ms. Jones. We've been under a lot of stress with all the budget cuts lately, and I'm sure he didn't mean any disrespect." She turned to Hopkins before continuing. "Did you, Bill?"

He dropped his arms to the side, hooking his thumbs in his pockets and lowered his head. "Sorry, ma'am, it's been a tough week." It was obvious to everyone, including Fred, who was at the top of their pecking order. I swear I saw Fred smile.

Cruz turned to me, unconsciously patting the front of her blazer. "What about this letter, Jake? Did you find it there, too?"

"Did Lisa tell you about that?" Bonnie looked around the room the way someone scans the passengers deboarding a plane. "And speaking of her, where is she?"

Cruz looked over at Bonnie. If she was upset about the interruption, she didn't show it. "Yes, she did, Ms. Jones, but not until I told her about the other letters. That's when she mentioned how Jake pretended to be looking for his saw and she saw him put what looked like a letter into his pants. And if you must know, she couldn't make it, something about seeing her lawyer, which is why I asked Jake to come down and show us where he found the letters." Then she turned back to me. Her face was as readable as the terms of a service agreement one clicks on when they install a new app.

"Now if your partner doesn't have any more questions, perhaps you wouldn't mind answering mine," she said with a smile phonier than Ronald McDonald's.

"I'm sorry, Sarge. I forgot the question."

Her eyes narrowed her smile vanished. "Is that where you found the letter? And please don't call me that," she said pointing to the holes in the wall.

"Sort of," I answered. "The other letters were in the armoire which used to be there. The last one was just sticking out of that hole next to your sergeant. I found that strange."

"Why's that?" Hopkins asked. "And where is this armoire you mention?"

"I assume it's on the way to Loveland by now. Lisa said she sold all the antiques to a dealer up there."

Hopkins pulled out a notebook from his sportcoat pocket and started writing. "Do you know the name and address of this dealer?"

"I already got that from Ms. Carpenter, Bill," Cruz cut in before turning to me. "So why do you think finding the letter where the armoire was is strange, Jake?"

Her eyes looked like they could see into my soul. "Well, it's strange I didn't find it when I moved the cabinet."

"Right," Hopkins said. He had been furiously writing down everything I said.

I ignored him and tried giving Cruz my own version of a mind-reading stare. "You said you'd tell me who told you about the letters."

The corners of her mouth raised a millimeter, and I thought I saw a spark behind her dark, penetrating eyes. "A little birdie, Jake. A cute little Robin, I think it was."

Bonnie's ears turned red and it looked like she was going to explode.

Cruz must have noticed. "Don't blow a fuse, Ms. Jones. I was only joking." Then turning to me with a smile only Morticia Addams could conjure. "If you two would come into my office on Monday to sign an affidavit, I'll tell you then."

***

"That's weird, Jake," Bonnie said as she pulled away from the curb at Debbie's house.

"What's weird, Bon. Lisa not showing up, or Cruz knowing about the letters?"

"Well, that too, now that you mention it."

"Then it was Lisa not showing up that you think is strange?"

Bonnie rolled her eyes at me. "That's not what I meant, silly. It's the kids. Didn't you notice all the costumes? It's Halloween and yet not one of them went up to Debbie's neighbor."

"They didn't come to Debbie's while we were there, either, Bon."

Bonnie stopped to let a ghost and a pirate cross in front of us. "Of course they wouldn't go there. Not after the murder, but why skip the neighbor?" she asked after the kids had safely crossed the street and she'd started to move again.

"Murder? I do believe the word on the street is that Debbie had a fatal accident. But as for the neighbor, they all think she's crazy. Remember when I told you some kids came up to pet Fred when I was sitting on Debbie's porch? They said she poisoned their dog when she caught it in her yard. I'm sure the parents won't let them anywhere near the place."

She nodded her head as if she agreed. We made it through the neighborhood and onto Colfax before she spoke again. "I think she likes you, Jake."

I was watching for more ghosts and witches, so I didn't turn when I answered. "Who likes me, Bon?"

"Sergeant Cruz, silly. Who did you think I was talking about? The crazy neighbor?"

"No, I've never met her." I didn't mention my mind was on Lisa.

"I wonder what she looks like."

I knew Bonnie well enough to know we were back to the neighbor. "I have no idea, Bon, but I guess her to be about Debbie's age."

Bonnie suddenly turned toward me, taking her eyes off the road. "Maybe it's her, Jake?"

"Incoming at three o'clock, Bon." The car pulling out of I-Hop looked like it wasn't going to wait for us to pass. Luckily, Bonnie was facing me and saw it, too, just in time to slam on her brakes.

She gripped the wheel so tightly that her knuckles turned white. "I saw him, sonny, and the last thing I need is a back-seat driver." Then she honked her horn and gave the driver a one-fingered salute.

I turned to the back seat where Fred had been sound asleep before the sudden stop. "You okay, Freddie?" Bonnie hadn't been going fast enough to knock him from his seat, but it did wake him.

She quickly glanced back at Fred before easing the Cherokee back into traffic. "Can you believe that idiot?" Then without missing a beat, "She sounds crazy enough to do it."

"Are we back to Crazy Mary?"

She didn't turn to answer this time, but I could see her eyebrows rise. "Of course. Who else would I be talking about?

"She has no motive, Bon. At least none that I can think of."

"Since when do crazy people need a motive? She probably did it during some stupid argument."

"I suppose it's possible. But unless Brendon, or someone else, wants to pay us to find who killed her and Ryan, I need to concentrate on more important matters, like finding a job before Fred runs out of dog food."

Bonnie gave a small laugh before speaking. "Are you forgetting Brendon already paid us?"

"Not at all. He paid us to find a letter. It may not be what he wanted us to find, but we did find one, so unless he's willing to pay to take it further, I need to get back to work."

"But you gave Cruz the letter."

I waited until Bonnie merged into the Sixth Avenue traffic before answering. Even though it was a Saturday, the traffic was stop and go. Fred didn't need to be jolted out of another nap. "Yes, I did. I guess Brendon will have to settle for a copy."

She didn't answer. Her full attention was now on the traffic. She was squinting so hard it made the wrinkles around her eyes more intense. When I saw her lower lip rise up to cover the top lip, I knew enough not to break her concentration. I turned around to check on Fred, then settled in for the ride home. We were about to merge onto I-70 traffic when I saw the Escalade.

Chapter Twenty

"That's him, Bonnie!"

Bonnie looked at me wide-eyed, then scanned the traffic in front of us. Her cloudy gray eyes seemed to clear up. "The Cadillac? Is that the one that caused your accident?"

"Yes. Can you follow him? He shouldn't recognize me in your Jeep. Stay back without making him suspicious, but get us close enough so I can get his license number."

"I will if this traffic would get going, Jake. Where did all these people come from?" Bonnie said, waving her hands like a banshee. "Why are they going so damn slow?"

Fred must have sensed the excitement in our voices, for he had his big head on our seat with his butt firmly planted in the back seat. He let out a bark to let us know he was in the game, too.

"I think Beaver Creek opened last week, but it's a little late in the day to be heading for the slopes. There must be an accident up ahead."

"Well, I wish they'd get moving or I'll never catch up with that Caddy."

I opened my window and stuck my head out to try for a better view. "Probably this way all the way to the Eisenhower Tunnel," I said after closing the window before Fred could stick his head out, too. "I imagine they got snow up there, and someone who doesn't know how to drive in our weather slid off the road."

Bonnie snorted. "One of those out of state idiots, I'll bet. They fly in from California or someplace where it never snows and think they can drive like they're back home."

"Tell that to the Donners, Bon."

She turned to look at me like I'd lost my marbles.

"The Donner Party? You said they never get snow in California. If I recall my history, those poor people were stuck in it for months."

"You know what I meant, smartass." She was interrupted by a car horn before she could say more. Bonnie showed them her middle finger before moving another ten feet forward and stopping again.

"I'm never going to get close enough at this rate, Jake."

"Not to worry, my dear lady. All I need is a clear shot," I said, taking my cell phone out of my pocket. "If you can get into the far left lane, I'll snap a picture of his car with my smartphone. It'll let me zoom in close enough to see the sticker on his plate if we want to."

Bonnie jerked the wheel to the left and cut off a driver who had been too slow to close the gap. He wasn't happy and leaned on his horn. Bonnie smiled at me and showed him her appreciation with her now famous, one-finger salute.

We were only one car behind the Escalade now, so I took several shots of the SUV and its driver before his lane started moving faster than ours and we lost him.

"Good driving, Danny," I said as I put my cell back in my jacket pocket.

We weren't moving, so I wasn't too upset when Bonnie turned her full attention toward me. "Who?"

"Danica Patrick. She's a famous race-car driver."

Bonnie laughed. "If you'd said Shirley Muldowney, I'd have known what you were talking about."

I felt like it was my turn to ask who, but let it go. "Why don't you get off at the C-470 exit and we'll take the back road through Morrison. I'd like to get home and call Julie's friend at the DMV to run the plate for us."

"Your wish is my command, Mario," she said, looking in her rearview mirror. "Why wait? Or does that fancy phone of yours do everything but make phone calls?"

"I don't have her number. It's at home, and who the heck is Mario?"

She simply smiled, reached over to rub Fred on the head, I assume for luck, cut in front of a semi, and headed for the right lane. There was no use trying to say anything over the blare of his air-horn.

***

It turned out to be too late to call Julie's friend at the DMV by the time we got back to my house, so I brought my laptop to the kitchen table to examine the pictures in greater detail. Bonnie had been in no hurry to go home and headed straight to my kitchen to see what she could 'rustle' up for us to eat.

Fred had had enough of being cooped up and gone off into the hills to do his thing.

Bonnie found a can of something in the cupboard next to my refrigerator. "How old is this hash, Jake?"

"Beats me," I said, looking up from my computer. Although I had several windows in my kitchen, the sun had just set, so the only light was from a ceiling light behind her. She had her hair in a ponytail, the way Julie used to wear it most of the time, and I suddenly had a shot of déjà vu mixed with a jigger of melancholy. Her profile looked like one of those caricatures drawn by a carnival artist. It dawned on me that Julie had put the can of hash in my cupboard only weeks before she had died.

"Are you okay, Jake? You look like you've seen a ghost."

Fred scratched at the door before I could answer. "I better let him in before he breaks down the door, Bon," I said, getting up from the table and turning away from her. I waited until I was at the door before wiping my eyes.

Fred rushed past me, heading straight for Bonnie, who was still holding the can of hash. He must have thought it was for him. It only made matters worse, so I went out on my front porch to be alone. Julie used to spoil Fred with canned dog food.

"Are you okay, Jake?" Bonnie had followed me out. I'd barely had time to sit in one of the two rockers I had on my porch when she appeared with Fred close behind. Fred must have sensed my mood and came over to sit by me. He put a paw on my leg, forcing me to stop rocking and look down at him.

"I'm fine, Bon. I just needed to clear my head," I said as I ruffled Fred's fur.

She took the other chair and started rocking back and forth. "Have you ever thought about selling these on eBay?"

I looked up from Fred who was in doggie heaven from the ear scratching he was getting. I was about to ask 'Sell what?'" when she continued.

"I'll bet you could get at least a hundred a piece," she said, turning a pack of cigarettes end to end. The way she slowly flipped them was mesmerizing.

"Go ahead, Bon. You deserve to light up after that drive on I-70."

"I'm serious, Jake," she said, pulling a cigarette from the pack. "I think you missed your calling. How long have these chairs been sitting out here? Two years? And they look like the day you made them."

I waited for her to light up and take a deep drag before answering. "That's because I put them in my shed during the winter and give them a coat of fresh stain every spring."

Bonnie raised the cigarette to her mouth and took another drag. It was like watching a miniature torch light up the wrinkles of her face. "Well, I better get back to fixing dinner," she said, dousing her cigarette in a beer can on the little table between the chairs. Although I didn't drink anymore, I had left the can there for her from when I did.

Fred looked up from his ear massage as if to ask permission to follow her. I quit rubbing his ears and nodded for him to go after her. "Go on, you traitor. But you're going to be in for a big shock when you see that can isn't dog food."

***

Bonnie left shortly after dinner. Calling it dinner, though, would be like calling a McDouble a feast. Still, Fred didn't seem to mind when he not only got his share, but most of ours as well. He was sound asleep at my feet by the time I finally got around to booting my computer.

I wasted several hours trying to connect the license number from the pictures I took of its driver. At first I ignored all the pay-to-see sites by using the term 'Free' in my searches. When that didn't work, I tried searching several Colorado government websites, including the DMV. I discovered that information required me to fill out several forms that included the VIN and the owner's name. Then I had to either take it to their office in Lakewood, or send it to the main office in Denver. Either way, it would take three weeks at a minimum. I thought of Joseph Heller's novel, *Catch 22*. If I knew the owner's name, why would I bother with the request?

Finally I gave in, and went to one of the pay-per-search sites. Poor Fred got startled out of a sound sleep when I slammed my fist on the table and let out a few cuss words I thought I'd forgotten. After paying nearly ten dollars for the information, they said they would email me the results in three business days. This was Saturday. I wouldn't get results until Wednesday or Thursday. By that time, the driver could be in Rio. I almost wished I had a beer in the fridge.

Fred soon decided I wasn't going to shoot him and laid back down. Within minutes, his eyes were racing a hundred miles an hour indicating he gone into a deep sleep, but by that time I'd seen enough of the driver from my pictures to know I wasn't going to need to wait for the online service to run a trace on the license plate.

Chapter Twenty-one

I waited until the Sunday services were over before breaking the news to Bonnie. It had been too late to call her the night before and I didn't want to upset her before church. I had been going to her church most Sundays, ever since Julie died. We were in the church basement where several of the congregation gathered for coffee and donuts after the service. Poor Freddie stayed home and missed out on the donuts.

She had been listening intently with elbows on the table, holding her cup in both hands. "Why did you wait so long to tell me, Jake? This changes everything."

"I couldn't very well bring it up in front of all your friends. I had to wait until I got you alone."

"Are you sure it's Lisa?"

"Pretty sure. Here, take a look." I pulled my smartphone from my jacket pocket and opened the pictures of the Escalade."

She adjusted the rope holding her reading glasses around her neck, and put them on the tip of her nose. "It's too small."

"You can zoom in with your thumb and index finger."

She raised her eyes so she could see over her glasses without removing them. The look she gave me didn't require any words to make her point.

"Here, let me show you," I said, taking my phone back and zooming in on the picture for her before handing it back.

She adjusted her glasses again and looked down at the picture, then let them fall off her nose. "It sure looks like her, doesn't it?"

I reclaimed my phone before she had a chance to drop it. "Here's another," I said after swiping to the next picture and zooming in for her.

"I don't suppose you have any of her straight on? Oh, of course not, we would have had to get in front of her to do that."

"But I do, my fair lady. Look in the side mirror." I took the phone back, zoomed in further, and gave it to her again.

"My God, Jake! It is Lisa!" She suddenly realized where we were and clasped her left hand to her mouth. A couple at the next table looked over at us, and then went back to their conversation when Bonnie returned their stare.

We both pretended nothing had happened. Bonnie quietly sipped on her coffee while I took another bite of my chocolate-iced, cake donut. I wanted so badly to dip it in my coffee, but visions of my mother frowning stopped me.

Bonnie finished off her sugar donut and washed it down with the last of her sweetened coffee before speaking. It made me wonder if she would be a candidate for diabetes with all the sweets she consumed. "So what's next, Sherlock? Do we show these to Sergeant Cruz when we go see her tomorrow?"

"I thought you had to go back to Margot's tomorrow?"

"I'd rather have my toenails pulled out by the roots than miss seeing Cruz's expression when we tell her we solved the case."

I had to laugh. "Hold on my dear, Watson. Even if it is Lisa in that Escalade, how does that prove she murdered anyone?"

"She tried to kill you, Jake! It's obvious we were getting too close to solving the case!" Our neighbors stared at us and didn't bother to hide it. Bonnie showed some level of restraint, considering where we were, and only glared at them. I was confident she wouldn't salute with her finger, but I wasn't so sure she wouldn't stick out her tongue.

The couple looked away then gathered up their cups and napkins to leave. Bonnie turned back toward me, smiling. She started to say something, but stopped. Her smile went from one of those happy emoticons to a sad one. "Okay, so they don't prove anything other than she was driving a Cadillac Escalade. And we don't even have proof it was the same Caddy that tried to kill you, do we?"

"Exactly, Bon. I think it's time I went back to Debbie's and looked in her garage. If there is a Cadillac parked in there, I should have the proof I need."

"How's that, Jake?"

"There's a small spot of paint on my Wagoneer's front bumper. I must have tapped the rear of her car when she slammed on her brakes. If the paint matches, I can at least file a road rage complaint against her when I see Cruz on Monday."

Bonnie's posture stiffened and her blue-gray eyes turned a shade grayer. "You mean *we*, don't you? I told you, there's no way I'm missing out on this. Don't think for one minute that you're going back to Debbie's alone."

"Who said I was going alone? Are you forgetting Fred?"

"Of course not. But I'm part of this team, too, sonny, so I'm going. And that's that."

***

Bonnie gave me at least a hundred reasons why I couldn't check out the Cadillac Escalade without her on our drive back to my cabin to get Fred. Although there was no danger of him freezing or getting rained on, I didn't want to leave him out after dark.

Among some of her reasons were reminders of all the times she'd saved my rear on similar trips. I didn't mention that most of those times she had been more of a liability than an asset, but her most persuasive argument was that I needed her Cherokee. The broken taillight on my Jeep would certainly attract all kinds of cops, and more importantly, unless I parked a mile from Lisa's I might as well knock on her door and tell her we were there to inspect her garage.

"Okay, Bon, you win," I said when she pulled into my drive. Before she came to a complete stop, I felt a cold premonition sweep over me.

"What's wrong, Jake? You look like you've seen a ghost."

"He's not here, Bon. Fred is always here to greet me. Even when I'm gone ten minutes, he's jumping up and down and wagging his tail, like he hasn't seen me in a week."

My fear was contagious. Now it was Bonnie who turned white. She got out of her Jeep faster than I'd seen her move since I'd know her. "Freddie," she yelled at the top of her lungs. "Come to Aunt Bonnie, Fred!"

"Come on, Fred," I yelled a second later. "Come here, boy!"

We both stood still, listening and waiting. Nothing. Not a single bark or yelp.

"Why don't you drive down to your place, Bon, and see if he's lying on your deck? I'll check my deck. Call my cell if you find him."

Bonnie hesitantly opened the door to her Jeep. Her eyes were wet. "Only if he's down there, otherwise I'll be back in ten minutes with my hiking boots and a gun."

She knew me too well, for I had already planned on hiking up our little mountain to search for him, but the last thing I needed was a seventy-year-old woman with a gun following me up a steep mountain trail. "Leave the gun home, Bon. It's not a safari."

Her mood changed quicker than our weather. She stared at me like I'd called her every four-letter word in the book. "What if it's a cougar?" she said.

"Then your little pea shooter will only make him mad. I'll bring my dad's twelve gauge."

I'd been fighting back the image of dead llamas I'd seen in our local paper a few months back. The murder scene was on the other side of the hill behind my cabin, in a meadow once owned by Willie Nelson. They had been slaughtered by a mountain lion. He, or she, had done it just because he could. He obviously hadn't been hungry, for once the animals were dead, he left them where they fell. They had been penned up and didn't have a chance. At least Fred had a chance, as I never tied him up, but it wouldn't be much of a chance with a cat three times his size.

***

The trail up the mountain was nothing more than an old animal path that wound back and forth, and had been slightly improved over the years by hikers who had cut and removed dead trees that had fallen across it. We were halfway up the hill when Bonnie stopped to rest. "You should have brought him to church, Jake. No one's ever complained before." I hadn't noticed her red eyes on the way up because she was behind me.

"Now I wish I had, Bon. It was such a nice morning, I didn't have the heart to keep him on a leash during the service."

"You don't think the mountain lions got him, do you?" she asked, then started to cry again.

"No, I don't think so. We would have seen some sign of a struggle by now."

She wiped her tears and stood up. "I'm just holding you back. You go on without me and I'll check with the neighbors to see if they heard anything."

"Thanks, Bon. I don't think the Clarks were home at the time. I didn't see any cars in their driveways when we drove by, so you might try the other end of our circle. Maybe the Simpsons are home."

She looked down the hill for confirmation, even though it was impossible to see any of the neighbors through all the trees, and then turned back to me. "Call me if you find anything, Jake."

I nodded my head.

"Promise."

"I promise, Bon," I said, then headed up the trail.

***

Fred and I had climbed this trail so many times that we both knew it better than any street in Denver. The trail was part of the Denver Parks System. There were over five thousand acres of undeveloped, landlocked wilderness behind my cabin whose residents included mountain lions, black bear, deer, elk, coyotes, raccoons, and several rodents. I'd never seen a snake or another human on any of the hikes we took. Unlike the woods we'd seen a few years back in Missouri, Colorado forests are not that dense. Fred used to leave the trail at several places whenever he smelled an animal's den, or chased a squirrel. It was at one of his favorite side trails that I saw long scratches on a nearby aspen. At the base of the tree were the unmistakable remains of an animal carcass.

The scratches, I knew, had been made by a black bear. I don't know if they do it to mark their territory or what, and at the moment, I didn't care. My heart was pounding, and the thin air was starting to get to me as I got closer to examine what I prayed wasn't my best friend.

I was near tears when I realized the body belonged to some unfortunate raccoon and heard Bonnie call out. "Jake, get your butt down here! I think I found something." I didn't waste any time with the switchbacks and ran straight downhill, falling and sliding on my rear more often than not.

"What is it, Bon," I asked between gasps of oxygen when I got to the road.

She waved a piece of yellow celluloid in my face that I immediately recognized.

"Brendon? You don't think…"

"Who else do we know that's addicted to butterscotch candy? His car's floor must be littered with them, and this one fell out when he took Fred." She was bouncing from foot to foot and waving her hands like one of those sailors signaling an incoming jet on an aircraft carrier.

"He'd never get in the car with Brendon, and I doubt very seriously if he took Fred, but I wouldn't be surprised if Freddie chased him all the way down to Upper Bear," I said, after we had walked a few yards back to my cabin.

Bonnie sat down on the porch steps, pulled out her cigarettes and lit one. "I hope he didn't go down there. He'll get run over on that road the way people drive."

She got up suddenly, and stomped out her cigarette. "I'm getting my Jeep and checking it out."

I barely had time to say anything before she took off for the path between our houses. "Come get me, Bon. I'll throw on a sweatshirt and join you." I could only assume she heard me, for she was gone before I finished speaking.

I raced up my porch steps and headed for the door, then froze. Sticking halfway out from under Fred's water bowl was a piece of paper. I didn't need my magic eight ball to tell me what it was.

Chapter Twenty-two

I picked up the note from under the bowl. It was written in perfect cursive, but so small that I had to squint.

Jake, Fred is okay and will be returned as soon as I get the letter. If you'd be kind enough to put it back where you found it tomorrow, I'll make sure Fred finds his way home. Put an ad on Craigslist under 'Wanted' saying you lost your wallet after you've returned the letter.

Bonnie came roaring into my driveway the second I finished the letter. "Come on, Jake! Let's go," she yelled.

I slowly walked over to her Jeep holding the note in front of me like a white flag. "Turn off the engine, Bon, and come inside. Fred's okay–I think."

***

Bonnie read the note again, for the tenth time, before handing it back to me and picking up her glass of Jack Daniels. "That blows my theory about Brendon. This note was definitely written by a woman, just like the last letter you found. Can I see that copy, Jake?"

"You're telling me men can't write cursive that well?" I asked, getting up to fetch the letter for her from my kitchen junk drawer.

She leaned back in her chair. "You bet they can't. In all the years I taught school, not once did I ever have a male student who could write like that."

I had to agree with her, but didn't say it out loud, and handed her the letter.

Bonnie refilled her glass from a half-empty bottle she had kept in her Jeep for emergencies, before adjusting her reading glasses. She still had to squint while she compared the letters. "Well, either Brendon went the way of Bruce Jenner, or he has an accomplice. These were definitely written by the same woman. If you ask me, he and Lisa are in it together."

Her remarks had barely registered, for I couldn't get the picture of Fred being tied to a tree or locked up in someone's basement out of my mind. "I'm not waiting until tomorrow, Bon."

She set her glass down and stared at me.

"I *can't* wait until tomorrow. If it *is* Lisa, then chances are she's got Fred with her at Debbie's house. He's probably locked up in the basement with a muzzle to keep him quiet."

***

Bonnie parked across the street from Debbie's pretending to read a map, while I checked with my binoculars for any signs that Lisa was in the house. I could only hope the dome light didn't give me away, too. The house was completely dark; not so much as a nightlight could be seen. If Lisa was there, she had to be asleep. Then I checked out the neighbors' houses. The house on the right had several lights burning in the lower level, and I could see the distinct glow of a TV in one of the upper bedrooms. Crazy Mary's, on the left, also had a light on in what I assumed was an upstairs bedroom.

I looked over to Bonnie who was still acting the charade of being lost. It was a good thing nobody could see her, because she had the map upside down. "I think if we go around back to the alley, Bon, we might get away without being seen."

She started to fold up the map and was getting frustrated that she couldn't get it to bend where it wasn't supposed to. "What about the house on the right, Jake. Won't they see us?"

"No, not unless someone is in one of the back bedrooms. The hedge between the houses will block the view from anyone on the lower level. We just need to be extra quiet."

She gave up on the map and threw it in the back. "Why can't they make these so it doesn't take a contortionist to fold them?" she asked and started the Jeep.

I tried to sneak a peek at the houses with lights still on to see if we were being watched as Bonnie slowly drove down to the corner and turned left. Her dash clock said it was half past nine. Maybe, with a little luck, it was still early enough that anyone watching wouldn't think we were burglars and call the cops. Another left turn put us in the alley behind Debbie's house. Alleys in this part of town were designed to split the block in half and put the garages in the back where they couldn't be seen. Evidently, garages were considered eyesores back in the early twenties. The garages weren't marked, but I knew which one was Debbie's and had Bonnie pull up next to it. I figured we had twenty or thirty minutes before someone reported us. There were NO PARKING signs posted on every telephone pole.

Most of the garages were narrow and made to house a single car. They were built on the property line with five-foot, cedar picket fences enclosing the remainder of the yard. Debbie's fence was still stacked in a pile where I'd put it when they brought in the dumpster.

"What do we do now, Jake?" Bonnie asked after we left the Jeep and walked past the garage toward the house. "Are we going to break in? What if Lisa's in there? What if..." We both stopped dead in our tracks.

"Is that Fred?" Bonnie asked when we heard a dog barking inside Debbie's garage.

"You bet your life it is. I'd know his bark anywhere!"

I didn't wait for Bonnie and ran over to the side door of the garage and kicked it in. Fred was on me in a second, knocking me off my feet, and licking my face. I swear I heard him cry.

We were lying on the grass by the side of the garage when Bonnie caught up with us. Fred stopped kissing me when he saw Bonnie. Fortunately for her, his energy had been spent on knocking me to the ground and he didn't do the same to her. "Oh, Freddie, you had us so worried." I could see tears running down her cheeks, even in the dim moonlight. She bent down on one knee and took his big head in her hands. "What is this?" she asked, noticing a shredded muzzle hanging from his neck.

I bent down to take a closer look. Someone had indeed muzzled him, and he had managed to tear it off his snout, leaving it to swing from his neck. I reached over to unfasten the Velcro strap, but was interrupted before I could get it off completely.

"What's going on, Jake?" I looked up to see Lisa standing over me with a baseball bat.

"Put the bat down, Lisa." Bonnie reached into her jacket pocket and pulled out her cell phone. "I've got one-touch 911 dialing. Put it down, or I call the cops."

Lisa turned to Bonnie, jabbing a finger toward her face. She was literally shaking, and raised the bat higher. "You're calling the cops? I'm the one who should be calling them!"

Fred came over to me with his tail between his legs and his ears pinned back. I reached down to comfort him. "It's okay, Freddie. I won't let her hit you."

Lisa must have realized how the bat and everybody's tone had affected Fred. She dropped the bat and went over to him. "Oh, Freddie. Did I scare you?" she said, bending down on one knee to pet him.

"What's this, Jake?" she asked when she saw the muzzle. "Did you muzzle him to keep him quiet while you broke into my sister's house?"

Bonnie put her phone back in her pocket and looked at Lisa wide-eyed. "You didn't do that?"

"Me? I wouldn't hurt him for the world."

"Then how did he get in your garage, and what are you doing here, anyway? I thought you had to get back to your job in Kansas City?"

"Not that it's any of your business, but Brendon asked me to stay until it's okay for him to list the house. Now do you mind telling me what you two are doing here?"

I thought I'd better answer before Bonnie did any more damage. "Fred was kidnapped earlier today and the ransom note led us here. I'm sorry about the door, but it's just the jamb and I can fix it like new."

Lisa gasped and stared at me like I'd said I just killed someone. "Kidnapped?"

"The note was written by a woman," Bonnie said. "She wanted us to return a letter Jake found in your sister's house, so we put two and two together..."

"And came up with five." Lisa cut her off, and finished the sentence for her. Then she turned toward me with hurt written all over her face. "You really thought I'd kidnap Freddie?"

Fred's tail popped out from between his legs and started wagging at the mention of his name. Lisa's tone of voice must have also helped. She looked down at him and smiled. "I would never hurt you, would I Freddie?" Then she turned back to me. "Why don't you guys come inside and tell me all about it? I've got a bottle of chardonnay in the fridge for me and Bonnie, and I can put on a pot of coffee for you, Jake."

"I've something a little stronger in the car," Bonnie said, and started toward the gate. "Go ahead, Jake. I'll be with you guys in a couple minutes."

"We'll be next door, Ms. Jones."

Bonnie and I both stopped dead in our tracks. "Next door?" I asked.

"Yes. My neighbor is out of town and asked if I'd house sit for her cats. Deb's house gives me the spooks, so I jumped at the chance."

***

"So how long have you been watching the house?" My question was meant as small talk while Fred and I sat in Crazy Mary's kitchen, watching Lisa grind some coffee beans in an expensive looking grinder.

She answered without turning around. "Since I got back from Kansas City last Friday."

"So that's why I saw you run over here after kissing me?"

This time she stopped what she was doing and turned around. She held her head down when she spoke. "I'm sorry about that, Jake. I don't know what came over me."

"I'm the one who's sorry, Lisa. You have no idea how much I wanted to follow you."

"Really?" she said, looking up from her study of the floor tiles.

"Yes. Until I started feeling guilty when I realized how much you reminded me of my Julie."

"Julie?" she asked. I could see the muscles tighten in her forearms when she crossed them in front of her chest.

"His wife." Bonnie had come into the kitchen so quietly that no one but Fred had noticed. If I'd been more observant I'd have seen him wagging his tail.

Lisa dropped her arms and turned back to the coffee grinder. "Do you always listen in on private conversations? You could have at least let us know you were here." Then without any warning she slammed the bag of beans on the counter, sending them flying.

Her outburst startled Fred. She turned in time to see him hide behind me. If it bothered her, she didn't show it. "Please leave," she said and started crying.

I walked over to her and put a hand on her shoulder. "Lisa, I'm sure she didn't mean to listen to our conversation."

She pushed away and simply glared at me. Her nostrils were enlarged to the point I had an insane image of a fire-breathing dragon. "Do I have to call the cops and tell them you broke into my sister's garage?"

"And we'll tell them why!" Bonnie yelled back.

This time, I reached out for Bonnie, afraid she was about to start round one of a cat fight. "Let's go, Bon. We've found Fred, so we're finished here."

***

Bonnie didn't speak a word until she turned onto Sixth Avenue. "I wish the Cadillac had been in that garage, Jake."

"Aren't you glad we got Fred back?"

She took her eyes off the road to answer me. "Of course I am."

I instinctively reached for the steering wheel when she started to drift. I could have let it go as there wasn't any traffic close to us, but instinct is more powerful than reason.

She swatted my hand away and went back to driving. The silence didn't last nearly long enough. "She's playing you like a banjo, you know."

"You mean fiddle, don't you?"

Once again she gave me her undivided attention. "What?"

"The expression, Bon, it's played like a fiddle," I said nodding toward the road.

"Whatever," she said and jerked the Jeep back into our lane.

I waited until she had safely merged onto I-70 before speaking. It looked like she had calmed down with the help of a cigarette she had lit a few minutes back. "Maybe it was, Bon."

She couldn't take her eyes off the road this time, for traffic was heavier now that we were on the major road going to the ski resorts, but I could imagine the face she was giving me. "The Cadillac, Bon. We should have checked Crazy Mary's garage."

Bonnie pushed her window button so she could throw out her cigarette butt. I welcomed the momentary fresh air and held my tongue about the dangers of forest fires. "The thought that she was driving Crazy Mary's car never occurred to me. Should we go back and check?" she asked.

"Not tonight, Bon. It's been a long day. And even if the Caddy is there, I don't see what we can do about it. I'm more concerned about finding the creep who kidnapped Fred than confronting Lisa over a fit of road rage."

"I guess I was wrong about her writing the forgery and the kidnap note, huh?" she said without taking her eyes off the road. "It's looking like I was right the first time. It has to be Brendon."

"Those butterscotch wrappers do point to him, but I still don't think he wrote the note or the letter. There's no doubt they were written by the same person, but why would Brendon plant a letter that does nothing to invalidate Debbie's claim? On the other hand, Lisa is in line for an Academy Award if it's her. I only wish I hadn't ticked her off again. I'm sure she could have told us something that would lead to Fred's kidnapper."

"She *is* emotional, isn't she? But from what you told me about Debbie, I guess it runs in the family. Or maybe it's the water. Is the whole neighborhood crazy?" she said before having to slam on her brakes.

"Damn, Jake. Can you believe the traffic this time of night?"

"There must be an accident in the eastbound lane up ahead. It's probably rubberneckers."

"Yeah, I forgot how bad it is coming back from the mountains on a Sunday. I think I heard they expected ice on the roads up there today."

It's a good thing Bonnie couldn't see my mouth drop open. It might have made her swerve into another lane. Suddenly, I realized who killed Debbie.

***

We were on Evergreen Parkway before either of us spoke again. I didn't want to say anything about my new theory until I'd worked it out. Even Fred had lost interest in our conversation and was sound asleep in the back seat. Bonnie broke the silence just as she passed Bergen Park. "I can drive by there on my way to Margot's tomorrow."

I looked at her blankly. I had been so deep in thought about her last comment that I'd forgotten about the Cadillac.

"The Caddy, Jake. I'll check and see if it's in her garage on my way to Margot's"

"Please don't do that, Bon. If my guess is right, you could be putting yourself in a lot of danger."

"But we've got to know. I hope you're not going to let her get away with road rage, just because of one little kiss." Her eyes were off the road again. It was too dark to see her expression, but I could imagine it wasn't a happy face. "Someone needs to report her, so if you won't, I will."

"Okay, Bon. Don't blow a fuse. I'll check it out tomorrow."

She turned her attention back to driving when we both heard the thumping of those annoying road bumps on the side of the road. "Promise?"

"I promise, Bon," I answered, holding up my hand in a three-fingered Boy Scout salute.

She quickly glanced at my hand. "You were never a Scout, Jake. Cross your heart and hope to die, then I'll believe you."

I hoped she was joking and not becoming senile, for I hadn't had a conversation like this since I was ten. "Cross my heart and hope to die," I said.

"Good. But I'm going with you, just to make sure."

***

Bonnie dropped Fred and me off at our cabin, but not before making me swear for the third time that I'd take her with me when I went to check out the Cadillac. It's a good thing I never was a Boy Scout, because it was one promise I had no intention of keeping.

Although Fred had been rescued, I still needed to catch the dognapper, so I placed the Craigslist ad under the 'Wanted' category, claiming to be looking for a lost wallet. Unless the creep had been watching us, or had gone back to check on Fred, he would have no way of knowing he was being set up. Next, I called Sergeant Cruz and left a message on her voicemail telling her about the kidnapping. I also told her my new theory on who was doing all the murders, and how I planned to catch two birds with one stone. Now all I had to do was go back to Debbie's in the morning and wait for the dognapper to show his face.

Cruz called back in less than fifteen minutes.

Chapter Twenty-three

Fred sat next to me in the front seat when we quietly left the house in the morning. It was half past six, which I knew was long before Bonnie would be up. We both lived on the same circular road, she on the bottom and me at the top, so I took the left part of the road to avoid going past her house.

"Looks like we did it, Freddie," I said, once we left our road and turned onto the dirt road leading down to Upper Bear.

Fred barked. I thought he was agreeing with me until I saw Bonnie's Cherokee parked on the side of the road. She was standing outside her Jeep, smiling. "Good morning, Jake," she said when we pulled up alongside and I rolled down Fred's window. "I know you wouldn't leave without me, so I assume you must be out of coffee and are just making a run to Safeway."

I got out of my Wagoneer and went over to her. She was no longer smiling. "Please stay here, Bon. I'm going to try to catch the creep who took Fred, and it could get nasty. I would never forgive myself if you got hurt."

"Are you armed?" she asked.

The question caught me off guard. "He's a dognapper, not a killer. I don't need a gun."

The corners of her mouth turned up ever so slightly, forming a wicked grin. She looked around, the way one does to see if anyone is watching, and opened her purse to give me a peek of a shiny handgun. "And Hannibal Lecter is a vegetarian. All the more reason you need me and Mr. Colt here."

She didn't wait for me to answer, closed her purse, walked over to my Jeep, and got into the passenger seat with Fred.

***

I pulled into the alley behind Debbie's house and snuck around to the side door I had broken the night before. I almost expected to see the Cadillac, but except for some old furniture and boxes, the garage was empty. I stepped inside, afraid Lisa might be watching, and pushed the button on the wall by the side door to open the big door.

Bonnie was barely able to drive my Jeep inside, with all the clutter Lisa had moved out of the house. I pushed the button to close the door as soon as she was inside. She and Fred no sooner got out of the Jeep when we heard the sound of another car park outside.

"Everyone down. He's here," I whispered, and flattened myself against the wall behind the side door, so I wouldn't be seen when he opened it. I wasn't a second too soon. If my guess was right, he'd open the door to check on Fred. It would be the only chance I had to surprise him.

"What the..." he said when he saw my Jeep. I slammed the door back as hard and fast as I could, then ran out to finish the job. Ryan was sitting on the ground, outside the door, with both hands on his face trying to stop the flow of blood from his nose. I grabbed one of his hands, twisted his arm backward, and put him in an arm lock.

"Move an inch, asshole, and I'll break it. Nobody messes with my dog and gets away with it." I'd never been in a fight my in entire adult life, and couldn't believe that what I had read about subduing someone actually worked – until I looked up and saw Bonnie pointing her revolver at his face with one hand and holding Fred's collar with the other. Fred had his lips pulled back, showing his teeth, and growled like he wanted to kill Ryan.

It didn't take long for the commotion and noise to attract Lisa's attention. She came running out the back of Crazy Mary's house barely dressed. She quickly finished buttoning her blouse and tucking it into her cargo pants. "You just can't leave well enough alone. Can you, Jake?" She wasn't the least bit surprised to see Ryan.

"No, Lisa, or should I call you Mary? Not when someone messes with my best friend. You two really screwed up when you took Fred hostage."

Bonnie nearly dropped her gun. "Mary?"

I released Ryan's arm and answered "Let me introduce you to Mary Jane Mitchell, Bon, the granddaughter of our letter writer, for whom she was named."

Mary went over to Ryan who was now standing. His nose was still bleeding, so she ripped off part of her blouse and held it to his nose. "What did that monster do to you, baby?"

"A lot less than I would have," Bonnie said, before Ryan could answer. Then she looked back at me. "Do you want to tell me what's going on, Jake?"

I didn't get a chance to answer. Fred started growling again when the gate to the alley opened. "What's going on, Ms. Jones, is that you're going to drop the gun, or I'm going to shoot the dog and then you and Jake." Brendon's voice was steady and calculated. I wondered how long he'd been standing outside the gate, listening.

Bonnie looked at me with fear in her eyes. "Jake?"

"Better do as he says, Bon."

Ryan didn't wait for her to drop the gun and took it from her when she lowered it to her side. Then he turned toward me, and pointed it at my face. "I'm gonna blow your ugly face off, but first, you're gonna see what a broken nose feels like." He raised the gun to strike me with it when Brendon stepped in and grabbed his arm.

"Ow," Ryan yelled, "that's my sore arm."

"Go sit down, you idiot. Do you want every cop in Denver here when someone reports gunfire?" Brendon said, before turning his attention to me.

"How'd you know, Jake?"

"How'd I know Mary was pretending to be Lisa, or that you killed Lisa's husband?"

Bonnie came out of the shock she'd been in after having her gun taken from her. "What's he talking about, Jake?"

Now everyone was watching me, waiting for me to say something, even Fred.

"It's all the little things that didn't add up, like when I first met Mary when she was pretending to be Lisa. She didn't have a clue that the White Hawthorn Blossom was Missouri's state flower. That was pretty odd for a person who owned a flower business, but I didn't think too much of it, because it's not exactly something many people know, even people from Missouri. Then there were the initials on the walk board. I realized Debbie must have written MJM for Mary Jane Mitchell, and Fred, or the cat, had smudged the first letter, leaving JM. The kicker, however, was when you mentioned the icy roads on Loveland Pass, and how emotional Lisa was acting. The mention of ice triggered my memory of the frozen food Fred had found in Mary's trash." I stopped and turned toward Mary.

"That's where you put her, in your freezer, isn't it Mary?"

She gave me a smile that could scare Count Dracula, and nodded her head.

"And there wasn't enough room for her husband, so Brendon and Ryan took his body up to the Genesee rest stop after he started to smell."

"Great work, Sherlock," Brendon said. "But how did you know all that? About the body switch I mean?"

"That was easy. A child could have figured that one out. I called Cruz after Bonnie dropped me off last night to tell her about my hunch that Mary was impersonating Lisa. She let it slip that Ryan's dental records from all the expensive dental work he got for free during his first stay in prison didn't match the corpse. Then forensics was able to get a partial print off the burned corpse. They belonged to Robert Carpenter."

Bonnie cocked her head to the side and raised her eyebrows. "Why would he do that, Jake? He was set to inherit everything. Why would he want people to think he was dead?"

"Probably because he didn't want to spend the rest of his life in jail," I answered, looking at Ryan for confirmation. When I didn't get any, I continued, "The three strikes and you're out law, Bon. He already has two felonies for which he's spent a good part of his life in prison, and it was obvious to everyone that the so-called will is a forgery. It was only a matter of time before they charged him with another felony."

Ryan started screaming at Brendon. "I told you it wouldn't work, you stupid idiot! Shoot the bastard and let's get out of here before the cops show up!" He raised the Colt he'd taken from Bonnie and pulled the trigger.

Ryan's mouth fell open and he looked at the gun wide-eyed when it didn't fire. Fred was on him before he realized it was a single action and he had to cock the hammer for the trigger to work. He screamed when Fred's teeth tore into the flesh of his sprained arm. Ryan dropped his gun, causing it to discharge. A second later, Fred had him on the ground shaking his bloody arm like it was one of his pull toys.

As if on cue, I rushed Brendon, punched him in his gut, and grabbed his gun when he doubled over. It all happened so fast that both girls simply stood with their mouths open.

I slid back the slide to put a bullet in the chamber and pointed at Brendon's head. "Make one move for that gun Lisa, I mean, Mary, and your partner is dead meat." I looked over at Fred, who had firmly planted himself on Ryan's chest. He looked more like a Doberman Pinscher than a Golden Retriever.

"Bon," I said calmly, "would you be kind enough to pick up your gun."

She was on it in an instant, and held it in both hands, pointing it at Mary. I hoped the sirens we heard in the distance would get here before anyone realized the gun didn't have a round in its chamber.

Chapter Twenty-four

I pushed the garage door opener when I heard the first police car pull up. Almost instantly, the officer was out of his car, and hiding behind the protection of the open door. "Drop the guns and get down, now!" he yelled.

Luckily, Sergeant Hopkins was only seconds behind the first officer on the scene. He flashed a badge at the cop and took over. Cruz was right behind him. In less than twenty minutes they had Mary, Ryan, and Brendon in cuffs and on their way to jail.

Cruz came over to Bonnie, Fred, and me. We had been made to wait outside in the alley. "I don't know whether to shake your hand or cuff you, Jake. What were you thinking?"

"I don't know, Sarge. I was so mad at Brendon for kidnapping Fred. I guess I wasn't thinking straight. I didn't think Ryan and Mary would show up, too."

"It's Sergeant, Jake. I told you before, I'm not a drill instructor."

"He saved your butt, and that's all you can say to him? You should be giving him a medal." Bonnie evidently couldn't hold her tongue any longer.

Cruz smiled at Bonnie, and then knelt down to pet Fred. "The way I see it, big boy, if anyone gets a medal it should be you."

Epilogue

Fred never got his medal, nor did I. But like Sergeant Cruz said, we were lucky she didn't press charges for interfering with police business. The exact motive and means of why and how Debbie was killed came out when Ryan turned state's evidence on his partners to save himself from a life sentence. Mary had hit her over the head with one of my two by fours, and then finished the job with my bucket of drywall mud.

Ryan claimed it had been premeditated, because Mary hated Debbie and Lisa for what their grandfather had done to Mary's grandmother. He had raped her when she was a border and she couldn't live with the guilt, and killed herself soon after Mary's mother was born. Mary had bought the house next door and waited for the right moment to kill Debbie. Ryan had been using both Mary and Debbie and it all came to a head when Debbie found out Ryan was sleeping with Mary.

Mary then contacted Brendon and offered him a way out of his troubles. All he had to do was help her forge a will leaving everything to Ryan. The real Lisa and her husband were collateral damage when they showed up after Debbie died and caught Brendon and Mary in the house planting the forged will, so he shot them both in the head when they threatened to go to the police. Ryan showed up about the time they were stuffing the real Lisa in Mary's freezer. He had come to tell them the will was being contested and that he wanted out because he knew he'd be put away for life once it was discovered to be a forgery. That was when Brendon came up with the plan to switch bodies.

Everything would have worked out great, Ryan said, if Mary hadn't gotten greedy. She saw an opportunity to impersonate Lisa and claim the estate, which meant Brendon was back on the hook for two hundred grand. Things only got worse when he tried planting the forged letter that would disinherit her. So, in desperation, he kidnapped Fred, knowing I'd do anything to get him back.

Ryan's fate has yet to be decided, as is Brendon's. It will probably be another year before they go to trial and then with all the appeals, it could take years before they get what they really deserve. Mary, on the other hand, will probably never see the inside of a courtroom. She is currently under observation down in Pueblo, at the state mental institution.

***

Bonnie has been living with her sister for a couple of months now. Margot needed a triple bypass, and Bonnie's been with her ever since. I never knew how much she'd grown on me until she wasn't around anymore. Fred still goes down to her house almost every day. I kid him saying he's looking for a handout, but I know that isn't true, for I swear I see tears in his eyes at night when we sit by the pellet stove, watching the snow fall outside our window.

About the Author

Richard Houston is a retired software engineer who now lives on Lake of The Ozarks with a view to die for. He and his wife are raising their great-granddaughter, two Dachshunds, and a Golden Retriever.

If you enjoyed this book, please leave a review, and be sure to check out the others in the series:

A View to Die For

A Book to Die For

A Treasure to Die For

Or get the boxed set of the first three books:

Books to Die For

CPSIA information can be obtained
at www.ICGtesting.com
Printed in the USA
BVOW08s1830040418
512450BV00021B/779/P